TRIBESMEN

TRIBESMEN

ADAM CESARE

Prologue
The Island

The others, the strangers, were coming again.

Both the rafts and their passengers were small white dots on the morning horizon. Oroto paid them little attention and tightened his grip on the thatched mesh of the fishing net. His son Vatu stood further up the shore, paying no attention to what he was doing. His dark eyes were fixed out over the ocean, watching the pale men approach.

"Pick up your end! Stop staring at the boats and help me," Oroto barked, surprised at his own impatience with the boy. Every time they visited, Oroto's son was fascinated by the men and their peculiar rafts. Vatu's excitement would have to be curbed: this month over half of the village's crop had already failed. Fishing was the only way Oroto was going to be able to feed his family. His son could waste time later.

Besides the fact that their skin was the color of sand, their hair that of dead grass and their language unintelligible, there was nothing particularly novel about the men. The travelers were permitted to come ashore the island a few times a season to trade. Without a common language, the men were forced to gesture for what they wanted. The pale men's sign-language amused Vatu (and even some of the more 'mature' villagers) as they offered chickens and other less-than-useful trinkets in exchange for a place to sleep for the night.

Before the sun would rise the next morning, the men would be gone, embarking on the next step of whatever journey it was that they were making. Oroto didn't particularly care who they were or where they were headed, as long as they paid his people for the privilege to stop.

On behalf of the islanders, Oroto and his family were voted the brokers of these deals. Oroto was always glad to take the chickens, and his mother would then divide the rest of the take amongst the tribe. No one ever complained about the arrangement. The people of the island respected age, and there was no islander older than Oroto's mother. None of the islanders seemed to care much whether strangers bedded down on their meager piece of land for the night, as long as they weren't carousing or bringing their white devil gods with them off of their boats.

"Where are the chicken cages?" Vatu asked. He squinted against the light to make out the approaching visitors, shading his eyes with one of his small black hands.

"Maybe this time they will bring us fish," Oroto said, softening his chastisement. "We're going to need them, too, because I have a lazy son who catches nothing but sunshine and questions."

Vatu gave a short giggle before he went silent and returned to casting out the fishing net. The boy had caught a glimpse of his father's serious expression, and one stern look was all that Oroto needed to use.

The pale men were taking their time. They were not rowing yet, but instead allowed the ebb of the tide to pull them closer to the island. This was odd, but even more abnormal still was the large number of rafts they had arrived with today. Five hollowed-out crafts with three to four passengers each.

"The bones," a voice called from the end of the beach.

Oroto turned towards the jungle to see his mother

running out of the clearing. Puffs of sand flew up as she trudged down the upper part of the beach as fast as her gnarled legs could carry her.

Oroto let go of the fishing net and ran up the beach to meet his mother. As he closed the distance he yelled back to Vatu. He had to make sure that the boy brought in the rest of the fish.

His mother collapsed to her knees before he could reach her. Her small body was wracked with sobs as she writhed, clawing at the sand. Oroto placed one strong hand on her back, feeling the bumps of her spine as they jumped up and down with her cries.

"What bones?" Oroto asked, but he knew exactly what the old woman had meant. She had been up to her magic again. She used an odd collection of chicken bones and broken boar's tusks to look into the future. Or so she claimed.

She had collected the bones over her long lifetime, tossing them up into the air and making notes in the sand as to how they fell. With these bones she read the fortunes of the girls in the village. Normally, she used the practice to see who would be married and who would soon be pregnant: she was more of the village matchmaker than she was a psychic. The bones had never made her this upset.

"What is it mother? What did you see?" Oroto helped her to her feet and glanced back to see Vatu hurrying to gather up the net and the few small fish inside it.

Beyond the boy, he could now just make out the faces on the men in the first raft. Their faces were red, not the usual tannish-white. Also the men were rowing now, apparently no longer content to coast into shore.

"Call Vatu in to us," she said, and then she screamed out to the boy herself before Oroto had the chance: "Leave that, run up here!" Vatu looked at his grandmother, puzzlement etched into his face, then back to his father.

Oroto was hesitant to wave the boy in. Vatu held the net firmly in his grasp, reluctant to drop it before Oroto told him to do so. It would be a shame to waste the fish on the orders of a superstitious old woman.

"Please call him in," his mother said, squeezing Oroto's hand in hers. Oroto could feel the dry folds of her old skin, and her earnestness made his decision for him.

"Hurry up, boy," Oroto said, glancing beyond his son again, looking at the fast-approaching boatfuls of white men.

Then Oroto saw it. Blood. It was blood turning the white men red. They were covered in it from head to belly.

He then noticed that the lead man in the second raft was not a man at all, but instead a skinned corpse, propped up like a masthead. The corpse's skin was flayed, stretched across the back of the second raft and drying in the morning sun.

The men at the front raft were rowing with supernatural speed now. Seafoam frothed up from the ends of their oars and a fine mist enveloped the bow of their little craft. Behind them, the other four boats were following suit. There were never more than two rafts of white men at a time, but now there were five.

Vatu gathered up the net in both hands, juggling the two or three fish trying to flap their way to freedom. Oroto urged him on, and he dropped the net, beginning to run from the churning surf. Despite Vatu's constant insistence that he was nearly a man, the boy still had the ungainly waddling gait of a child.

His son was oblivious to the men that, a few minutes prior,he could not take his eyes off.

The men in the rafts were maybe twenty meters from shore when the first of them jumped off the side of his vessel. The big, bearded man splashed into the water. It was shallow enough to stand, and the line of the crystal blue water came up to the middle of his bloodied chest. The spot where he hit the waves immediately exploded into a cloud of burnished red.

The man screamed out in ferocity (or was it pain?) and began running. The waves sloshed against his face. The sea water cleaned off some of the blood, but the bearded man's skin was still crimson with sunburn and exertion.

As the second white man hit the water, Oroto sprung to his feet, intent on saving his young son.

Vatu must have seen the frenzy in his father's eyes, because he turned then, from his grandmother to the men coming up onto the shore behind him. "Father," the boy cried, breathless and terrified. The men left red streaks in the water as they closed the distance between their boats and the boy.

Oroto stopped, halfway between his son and his mother. The sun was so hot that it had turned the white sand of the beach into fire. It was the kind of flame that licked the bottoms of your feet if you did not move with enough haste.

The biggest man, the first off the boat, would be the first one to reach his son. Sea water, spittle and grue ran down his neck as he removed a large hook from the scabbard of his belt. The cast iron hook was the same kind they used to hang up pigs at the larger ports that surrounded their small island.

One disgusting white calloused hand grabbed Vatu by the shoulder, like a white scab on his beautiful, healthy skin.

The man's other fist brought the hook down, straight into his son's neck.

Oroto screamed, a wild sound. It was the sound a boar made when you had it cornered, the scream an animal makes when it knows that it's too late.

"Get up! We have to run!" Oroto shouted to his mother, as he raced back toward her. But he knew she could not run. He scooped one big arm around her waist and hoisted her up like a baby. She was not a little woman in her youth, but the years had dried and hollowed her like a prune. She weighed almost nothing in Oroto's strong arms.

"The bones, I have seen that there is no escape." Her voice was too calm. How could she be this calm after seeing what happened to her grandson? Oroto wanted to get to the village, rouse the men and kill these bastard invaders with his bare hands.

He could hear the pounding of footsteps behind him, and the laughter of the red devils as they nipped at his feet.

It happened too quickly after that. Oroto's left foot made an unlucky choice and disappeared into a deep hole in the sand, snapping his ankle. Some animal, maybe a crab or marmot, had dug the hole, and that hole had destroyed him.

The pain was excruciating, the sound of breaking bone loud enough to startle the jungle beasts. He heard chirps and cries as creatures rustled, fleeing deeper into the brush. Oroto made sure to toss his mother clear of his landing, extending his arms to try to cushion her fall.

The laughter of the men gave way to their dark shadows, spilling down upon mother and son. The hot sand burned Oroto's arms and stomach as he lay defenseless.

"You bastards," Oroto said, even though they would never understand.

One of the men put a soggy boot into the small of Oroto's spine. The laughing man pinned Oroto to the sand.

"Mother," Oroto said. The word came out a whimper. He had cried out for his mother in front of these men, these beasts that would kill a child.

His mother paid Oroto no attention; she was too busy scratching her ancient marks in the sand. The angular characters were ones Oroto had never seen her write. She spoke in the same clear, detached tone that she had taken to Vatu's death.

"I curse this place," she said. "I curse these men. I curse every grain of sand on this island. And I am ready to die."

They were the last words she ever said, and the last that

Oroto would ever hear.

> The white men gathered around their bodies.
> And painted themselves red again.

Chapter 1
Roland Pressberg
Executive Producer

A scream reverberated around the room.

The skinny redhead fell to her knees. She was surrounded by three nearly naked men. Over their dark skin, they wore a fine layer of gray ash, hair matted with clumps of dirt and mud. Their loincloths barely covered their buttocks, which quivered in anticipation of their next meal.

Grabbing at her tattered blouse, the center male gave a grunt of excitement. His hair was the dirtiest and his teeth were the greenest. This meant that the makeup girl had spent the longest amount of time on him, indicating to the audience that he was the group's leader.

After the men were done clawing away her undergarments, they set to work on her flesh.

"God damn it! Tito. Why do I have to watch this shit?" Pressberg stubbed out his cigarette and stared down at the ashtray on the coffee table in front of him. He had no desire to see whatever disgusting special effects the demented fucking Italians who made this shitty movie had come up with.

"But watch, this is the best part," Tito said. His English wasn't terrible, but his accent was laughable. His dialect was an inconsistent cartoon mix of Spanish, French and Italian. He held onto his 'e' sounds too long and put 'a' sounds on the end of words that didn't need them.

Tito's English was made impervious to criticism by the fact that he was also fluent in four other languages. Unless you could speak six languages to his five, you'd best leave his humorous pronunciation alone.

Tito pointed towards the screen as the film stained the walls of Pressberg's office red. Pressberg was dumb enough to look. The shot was a tight close-up of one of the ashy man's teeth as he squished down on one of the redhead's eyeballs.

Pressberg felt his stomach attempt a somersault.

"It looks fucking real," he said, suppressing a gag. "Are you sure it's even legal to be watching this in this country?" Pressberg hid his eyes in his hands again.

"No. Of course it's not legal in Portugal, are you kidding? Legal? *In Portugal?* Hah! All of this guy's movies are banned here," Tito smiled. "But don't worry: that's not a human eye. It's a goat eye. You can get anyone to eat anything, if you are having them eat it for the cinema. It is quite a neat trick."

Tito pronounced 'cinema' as 'chin-e-ma.' It was one of those holdovers from Italian that Tito kept consistent, no matter what language he was speaking. The word sounded pretentious, and Pressberg suspected that was exactly the way Tito liked it.

Tito Bronze had never been a name synonymous with art films. More like fuck films and exploitation garbage. It were as if the little man thought that by tossing in the word 'cinema' often enough, he could fool you into believing he was François Truffaut.

Pressberg was no longer even facing the screen, but he could still hear the munching of the three ashy men and the vaguely sexual moans of the redhead as she was torn apart. *If this were real life*, he thought, *she would be dead already, not coming.*

But it wasn't real life. It was the movies, and garbage like this played just as well in the Euro-markets (with a few cuts) as it did in America.

"Alright, I'll turn it off. Is that okay? Is that what you want, you big baby?" Tito asked, heaving himself up from the half-eggshell chair with both arms. Tito's open silk shirt billowed behind him like a cape as he rose.

The shirt was a disgustingly bright and brash floral pattern. Pressberg's father had been fond of saying that you could tell a lot about a man from the way he dressed. This meant that Tito was a clown.

"In business," Tito continued, "you are a very hard man, but in entertainment, you are as soft as her tits." Tito pointed once more to the screen, indicating the redhead's exposed breasts. They were slathered in fake blood so radiant and unrealistic that you could paint a barn with it.

"So this is it," Pressberg asked. His tone was not defeated, per se, just resigned. He didn't have to elucidate any further. Tito knew what he meant. What Tito heard was something like: *This is it? This is your next bafflingly profitable piece of shit? The next project I'm bankrolling?*

"This is it. A film for the eighties. A film for every market," Tito said, twirling the end of his off-white beard like some homeless magician.

"Except for Portugal," Pressberg said under his breath.

"To tell you complete truth," Tito said ignoring him, "I have already booked flight and put in order for equipment." Tito would drop articles from his speech when he was trying to get away with something.

"Booked a flight?" Pressberg said, concerned with where his money was quite literally flying off to. "A flight to where?"

"You never heard of it," Tito said. In twelve years of business, Pressberg had never refused to write a blank check for the director. Still, every time the funny little pervert tried to take more money from Roland, he wanted to snap his wallet shut and then bust Tito in the nose.

Tito must have sensed his agitation, because he added: "But this place is *bellissimo* and worth taking the flight. Caribbean Island. Pure and untouched by the cinema…and the fucking tourists. A dream location…and very cheap."

"Caribbean? I thought you said that this asshole actually filmed in the Amazon." Pressberg motioned at the projector to indicate that he meant the director of *Cannibal Fury Atrocity* (a direct translation from the original Italian title).

"Why shoot in Amazon when you can have palm trees with your jungle? Plus I no get eaten by fucking tiger or gorilla or some such shit," Tito said and smiled. The long slit of a grin exposed the dead teeth at the back of his mouth. "Plus there are primitives all over. The Amazon has no monopoly on savages."

"Fine, whatever. Bring it in fast and under budget. Don't let these Italians beat you to the punch with one more film than they already have. I'm sure those Guinea bastards have made three movies during the course of this conversation."

Pressberg put up a finger to signal that his terms were not yet finished. "Take the money, but promise me one thing."

"Anything for you, maestro."

"Promise that I never have to sit down and watch the fucking thing."

Roland Pressberg made a theatrical gesture, wiping his palms on his chest and washing his hands of this whole damn thing. He was Pontius Pilate with a checkbook.

"That's a promise, you big baby." The two men clapped hands. Tito was slick with sweat and nicotine stains.

As much as it pained him, they shook on it.

Chapter 2
Jacque Fuller
Screenplay

Umberto poked Jacque in the ribs with a strong, bronze finger and told him to get the blonde girl's attention. Jacque finished scribbling down the sentence he was working on before speaking to her.

"Pardon me," he said. He had to yell slightly to make himself heard over the plane's engine. "Umberto would like to ask you a question."

"Yes," she said, looking up and folding her glamour magazine against her lap. On the cover was Bo Derek's smiling face. Jacque had read that Bo was following up *10* with a Tarzan picture. That was probably not a great idea.

Umberto reached across Jacque and offered the woman a pocket mirror with three perfectly sculpted lines of powder across it.

"No thank you," she said, smiling wide. It was obvious that she was not looking to make a bad first impression.

With looks like hers, bad first impressions were practically impossible. She had the dimpled face of the all-American girl-next-door combined with the milk chocolate complexion of an African goddess. The blonde hair was from a bottle, but somehow it suited her.

She was still smiling as Umberto pushed the mirror closer. She was being too polite. This wasn't going to be a long shoot, but Jacque guessed by looking at her that she was a people-pleaser.

Umberto began speaking in Italian. The girl looked at him, puzzled, and then back down at the mirror which was still extended. The Italian's hands were shaking. Jacque decided to intervene before Umberto spilled the powder all over his lap.

"He says that it's not cocaine," Jacque said to the girl. "He's crushed up some downers and thought they might help you get some sleep on the flight."

"Could you tell him that it's alright? Tell him that I'm fine," the girl said and pressed Umberto's manicured hand, and the mirror, away.

Jacque told him and Umberto shrugged. The body-builder-turned-actor mumbled some things in Italian that Jacque thought it was best not to translate for the girl. The massive golden-haired Italian turned to the seat behind him and offered Daria, the makeup girl, a line before taking two big snorts and cleaning off the pocket mirror himself.

After five minutes, he was snoring, and Jacque couldn't decide which state of consciousness made the minor Italian movie star less appealing.

"What are you writing?" the blonde asked him. She was very pretty and only spoke English. Considering what he knew (that this was a Tito Bronze production and the fact that Jacque had never seen her before) he concluded that she was, in all likelihood, an American porno star.

"I'm writing the script," Jacque said, closing his pencil inside the notebook, ready to talk. The script was halfway finished and it was a long flight. He had the time.

"For this movie?" she asked. He watched her expression as her enthusiasm deflated. "The script for this movie isn't finished yet?"

"Yes, but don't look so surprised," Jacque said. "It's not that odd at all for these types of productions to still be writing up until the last day of shooting."

"Oh. Okay," she said unable to hide her disappointment. She had obviously been led to believe that this was a much bigger step up for her career. It wasn't.

"Don't worry though," Jacque said and reached out to pat the back of her hand. "I'll make sure that your lines are very good."

She smiled at him, but he could tell that he'd done little to assuage her fears. "I'm Cynthia, by the way." She gave him a slight but assertive handshake. It was an American shake to be sure. East coast, probably New York, he guessed. "Thank you for translating before. You speak Italian very well, but you don't sound it. Where is your accent from?"

"My name is Jacque. I grew up in Paris but studied in the UK." He assumed that she meant that he didn't look Italian either. She probably had not met many black Italians. He hadn't either, so he wasn't calling her a racist.

"Wow," she said. Her tone of voice suggested that this was her fist time out of the States, and it made him ashamed of his comparative jet-setting.

"Where are you from?" he asked.

"Queens," she said. "New York. What did you study in Britain?"

"English," Jacque said, ashamed also to admit to his education. "Literature. At Cambridge."

"You studied English at Cambridge," she asked and did not bother to hide her fascination or disbelief. "Then what the hell are you doing here?"

"Making a living," Jacque said. She went silent for a moment. It was his turn to ask a question.

"How long have you been acting?" Jacque asked and immediately regretted it. He had surmised that this was the girl's first feature after some 'modeling gigs.' Maybe a few sweaty casting sessions that never resulted in a callback. He had asked this question enough times to know the embarrassing silence it was usually answered with.

"All my life," Cynthia said, surprising him. "My parents were both theater people, and I've been in stage productions since I was an infant. I started out playing the baby Jesus in our church's nativity, and I've been going ever since." Her eyes lit up. He could tell that this was a monologue she'd delivered before, but she still enjoyed it. "I've laughed, sung, cried, tap-danced. Everything a person could do on the stage."

That was not the answer he'd been expecting. "What are you doing here?" he asked, but then shushed himself after seeing her piquant smile. "Never mind. You're making a living."

"Exactly," she said. "This may sound silly, but are all of us working on the movie?" She whirled a finger around in a circle, indicating that she meant the entire contents of the cramped charter plane. "I mean: are we all there is?"

"The whole kit-and-kaboodle," Jacque said, feeling like the cool man-in-the-know. "Hair, makeup, camera, lights. If it needs doing, there is someone in this flying shitcan that can do it. Pardon my language."

"Oh please," she said, the Queens-lilt busting out so she sounded like a New Yorker for the first time. "So who is he?"

She pointed to the unconscious Umberto. His upper lip and blonde mustache was quivering in his sleep, and there was a long string of saliva linking it to the lapel of his olive green leisure suit. He must not have been lying about the downers. They were probably the only way to get to sleep on the cramped, turbulent plane.

"That's Umberto Luigi. He also goes by Brent Cisco, his

American stage name."

"He can't speak English, but he has an American stage name?"

"Well doesn't he look American to you?" Jacque asked.

"His hair is blonde, but there's just something Italian about him. Some kind of extra quality," she said. She was the most polite and demure New York girl that Jacque had ever met.

"Could be that every time he exhales, my eyes tear up from all the garlic and bad cologne, couldn't it?"

She chuckled and covered her mouth the way Geishas in old Japanese movies did when they laughed. Jacque liked that. Maybe this job wouldn't be so bad.

"Hello, my darling." A thick plume of cigarette smoke heralded Tito's approach. Before the smoke had a chance to clear, he was leaning over Umberto's seat, his sweaty old-man gut pressing up against the big unconscious Italian's ear. "My exotic jewel, my starlet for a new age, my mulatto Fay Wray for the 1980s."

Tito's accent was in full swing, but his English was perfect. Jacque suspected that he turned it on and off at will. Tito sank down lower, going in for the kiss and spilling his drink onto Jacque's notebook. Cynthia offered only her cheek, not wanting to kiss the old Euro-pervert.

Jacque breathed a sigh of relief. He didn't think he could handle watching this lovely girl lock lips with Tito Bronze.

"Hey you, uh, Jacque," Tito said, pretending to forget his name and slurring enough that Jacque could tell he was halfway drunk. He cringed to think that he'd spent enough time around Tito (three films now) to tell when he was sloshed. "Where is Denny? I look everywhere for Denny. I want to talk about apertures, f-stops, light meters, all that shit."

If he was trying to impress Cynthia by discussing the finer points of cinematography, he was doing a terrible job of it.

"I don't know," Jacque said. The cabin was only about twelve feet long. Jacque made an exaggerated attempt to look for Denny, the cameraman, even turning around in his seat to check behind him. "I don't see him, do you? Maybe he's in the bathroom."

"That fucking kid has some kind of bladder problem. He's always on the shitter," Tito said. He took a sip of his scotch and then flashed a caustic smile back at Cynthia. "Ciao, bella," he winked and stumbled off to find his seat, fighting a losing battle against both the turbulence and his buzz.

Chapter 3
Dennis Roth
Cinematography

The touchdown of the small plane jolted Denny awake. The needle in his arm bobbed up and down until it finally clattered to the floor of the cramped bathroom.

He rubbed his eyes and then worked the strip of rubber tubing from around his arm into a loop and tucked it into his back pocket. After he daubed a bit of toilet paper against the flecks of semi-dried blood in the crook of his arm, he tried to stand. Failing, he flopped back down into his seat.

His closed his eyes for another moment, re-awoke to banging on the bathroom door.

"I'm coming," he yelled as he stood up from the toilet.

The water from the sink flowed out a dribble at a time and Denny was too impatient to fill his hands before wiping the few drops on his face and beard. He rolled his sleeves down over his pale skinny arms and buttoned the cuffs.

His shirt was sticking to his flesh. This was no good: he was already caked in sweat and he hadn't even stepped foot on the tropical island yet.

Around this time last year, he would have inspected himself in the mirror to make sure that he hadn't drooled down the front of his shirt, and paused to ask himself why he kept doing this. But he didn't even bother doing that much anymore.

Denny took a deep breath before undoing the latch and sliding the door open, shielding his eyes against the light of the cabin.

"Where have you been? Did you fall asleep?" Jacque asked, tossing him his duffel bag. "We're here and all the gear is already unpacked, so let's go."

Jacque knew. He had to have known. Jacque was a smart guy, even if Tito talked down to him and treated him like shit because he was a negro from France. Denny knew that Jacque could see the signs written all over his junkie face (never mind the occasional track mark that peeked out of his cuff). Knowing this made him feel nauseous, sicker than the trash had made him feel on an empty stomach.

The suspicion that he had been found out made him grip his duffel tighter against his chest as he stumbled towards the metal stairs that led off the plane. Trading the rancid, stale air of the cabin with that of the fresh sun-drenched island was probably exceedingly pleasant for everyone disembarking. Everyone but Denny. The light inside had bothered his eyes, but the light outside blinded him. The rays of the sun bounced up off the sand and sent flesh-colored bolts of pain shooting through his clenched eyelids.

Using the flimsy railing for guidance, Denny made his way onto the packed sand of the runway.

"Where are they?" Denny heard Tito's voice raise in indignant, impudent director-rage. Even when they aren't on set, directors think they can get away with anything if they use this tone. There was the screech of metal on metal from behind Denny. He concluded that the pilot must have been waiting for him to get off the plane so the crew could pull up the stairs.

"Where is who?" Jacque asked. Denny tried opening his eyes but the people around him on the runway were just five formless blobs.

"The fucking natives!" The shortest of the blobs waved its hands in exasperation. That one was Tito. Denny smiled through the pain that throbbed from behind his eyes down into his empty stomach.

He began to discern the rest of the shapes: Tito, Umberto, Jacque, Daria the makeup girl and Cynthia the new actress stood next to piles of their luggage and a few crates of equipment. Including Denny, there were six of them. The plane hadn't carried a full crew because Tito had insisted that they would be able to find cheaper labor on the island.

"They should have seen the plane land and come to meet us! Why do our modern wonders not thrill them? Where is our welcome party of savages?" Over the few years he'd been working with him, Tito had always found new and ingenious ways to outdo his own tastelessness. His blunt and hilarious lack of tact warmed Denny's junkie heart.

"You arranged for a welcome party of savages?" Jacque didn't sound half as amused by the idea as Denny was.

Umberto spoke up in Italian, momentarily breaking up the conversation. Denny could see fine now, and he could tell that the Golden Guinea was addressing Jacque directly.

He babbled for a while, peeling off his ugly green jacket as he spoke. The others turned in his direction. Denny and the new girl couldn't understand him, but everyone else on the crew spoke Italian.

"You want us to start walking to what camp?" Jacque said in English; he must have been translating for Cynthia's benefit. The pretty girl squirmed uncomfortably behind Jacque, looking down at her shoes and then back at Umberto.

"What do you mean there's no hotel?" Jacque's voice was raised to the point of yelling now. He walked up to the Italian, needing to crane his head to meet eye-to-eye. Umberto spoke some more and Jacque's expression blossomed into one of both understanding and despair. The actor was telling him something he didn't know. Denny thought that everyone had known that they were camping with the natives. The island didn't have a hotel.

"Hold on now. If I tell you, Mr. Prissy writer," Tito said, placing a hand on Jacque's shoulder before having it shaken off. "If I tell you that we're sleeping in native huts instead of nice fluffy hotel, would you have come?" Tito's arms contorted into an exaggerated shrug. "This way it is better, more authentic."

"Cheaper is more like it. And to answer your first question: no, I wouldn't have come." Jacque gave a look around. "So where are these natives, or how about just their 'native huts' for starters?"

Tito looked around and Denny looked, too. There wasn't much to see. Thick jungle surrounded both sides of the runway with a beach and the Caribbean Sea on either end. Behind them the plane was beginning its trek to the end of the strip, creaking on its landing gear like an oversized Volkswagen bus.

"Where is the plane going?" Jacque asked. The plane turned to face them on the far end of the runway.

"What, I'm a Warner Brother now? I buy private plane? No, I rent the plane."

"Well then, call it back, because I'm not staying here," Jacque said and turned to lock eyes with the blonde. "And I don't think the rest of you should either. This man is a huckster who probably won't even compensate you properly for your time. I'm quitting."

"Big talk from the big man. You want for me to call it back?" Tito usually spoke with less of an accent. He was done being cute. Denny didn't *like* Tito Bronze, per se, and he hated working with him, but some sick part deep down inside of him kind of admired the director's titanic stones. "Oh, I'll just call it back with my magic telephone that can place calls to airplanes."

"That is a real thing, you know. It's called a radio and I take it that means we don't have one."

"No, we don't. It will be back in three days, and in that time we will have enough footage for a film… as long as we shoot some filler when we get back to the city"

There was the sudden chug of an engine as the plane prepped for takeoff. Denny took a few steps forward, moving out of its path. He sidled up to Jacque and patted him on the back.

"I guess your resignation was rejected," Denny said. "Three days isn't that bad. It's not a lot of time to make a movie, but at least you won't starve. Buck up Jacky, m'boy."

"I'm not your boy," Jacque said. It was hard to tell if he was serious or not, so Denny just smiled. The six of them covered their eyes and noses in unison as the plane roared up into the sky, its engines whipping up a sandstorm to pelt them with dust and dirt.

After a moment, Tito coughed and spoke. "Denny, unpack the camera and pick up some footage as we walk up the beach. Alright everyone: let's make a goddamn movie," he yelled, the words pealing off into a hacking jag before he spit a glob of brown phlegm out onto the runway.

Chapter 4
Daria Casini
Makeup

How did I get here? Daria asked herself as she walked behind the group of movie-folk, the burning sand reaching up over her teal pumps and scalding the tops of her feet with every step.

Less than a week ago, when she had responded to an advertisement that read "makeup artist needed for film," she was sure she'd be turned down due to lack of experience. Daria was an ex-beauty student who was forced to turn freelance makeup girl once she had run out of tuition money. Modeling gigs had been sparse and film work had been non-existent.

That was until her meeting with Signore Bronze at his office in Rome (an office that appeared to have doubled as his hotel room). She suspected the interview went about as well as one could with Signore Bronze. Her prospective employer had never taken his eyes off her chest.

Two days later, she packed her small makeup bag of tricks and set off on this adventure to godknowswhere.

The whole thing would have been romantic if she wasn't so sweaty and tired from dragging her bags along the beach. Worse, the sun and sea-air had conspired to turn the slight curl of her thick black hair into a beachball-sized puff, making her feel even more out of place.

When she asked Signore Bronze what kind of movie it was going to be, Bronze had simply responded "a hit." Eavesdropping onto the writer's conversation during the plane ride had been just as useless. Jacque, the black French limey, was only interested in talking to the blonde black girl in English. Daria herself wasn't used to being snubbed by men, but that's the way it went when there was a blonde around. And in the rock-paper-scissors that was male attention, dark and gorgeous always seemed to beat olive-skinned and busty.

Daria had also tried asking the big movie star about it, Umberto Luigi, Brent Cisco, whoever he was, but he kept turning the topic of conversation to what color panties she was wearing. She resolved to minimize contact with the crew for the next three days.

"Look, over there! The path," Signore Bronze shouted in Italian. He was the fastest walker among them, probably because he wasn't carrying anything. "I told you."

The short man led the group up along the beach, insisting that the village where they would be staying had to be close to the airstrip. It wasn't, because the trip took about an hour. As they each hefted their personal belongings and equipment up the beach towards the jungle, Tito blocked their path to the shade of the treeline and lit a cigarette. He was no longer 'Signore Bronze' to her, never again after that hellish walk. Now he was simply Tito: an old man whose tacky floral print shirt was dripping wet, the armpits of his suit jacket a dark gray, and whose thin white pomp of hair was now matted against the side of his face.

Despite heaving for breath in the partial sunlight, Tito sucked in deep on his cigarette. Umberto shouldered his way past Daria, holding a large wooden crate and looking desperate for the cool of the jungle. When Umberto reached Tito the old man pointed his cigarette at him and put a hand down on the crate.

"Un momento," the director said with a slight wheeze.

In front of Daria, the writer translated his Italian to English for the two Americans, the actress and cameraman. "When we get there, the people will probably be… apprehensive. So everyone will let me do the talking."

Jacque rolled his eyes at this as he related it to the others. Tito clapped his hands and made an after-you gesture to the American and Italian blondes. Umberto grunted and pushed in front of Cynthia, hefting the crate into the shadows and leaning on it for a rest.

The hike through the jungle may have been slightly cooler, but it was made worse by the constant assault of bugs and the treacherous, narrow path. Daria tripped on an exposed root and went toppling into a deep mud puddle.

Umberto stopped in front of her, set down the crate and wiped the dirt off his pants before helping her to her feet. The actor didn't respond to her half-hearted "grazie." She was starting to think that he was nothing like his on-screen persona.

From up the path, Tito shushed her. "Listen!"

The crew held their breath. Daria found it difficult to stop her own panting in the afternoon heat. There was a snapping of twigs and some rustling of foliage in the distance.

"Hello? Is there anyone out there," Tito asked the trees. "It's okay, you can come out. We're from the cinema!" Daria wasn't sure if that last part made any sense, even if you spoke Italian.

Before she could further consider her newfound disappointment with the great auteur, there was more movement. Whatever was in the dark of the forest, it was closer this time.

Jacque said something in French, and Tito responded with Spanish vulgarity. Bronze was trying to sound tough, but his eyes were frantic and locked out onto the darkening jungle just like everyone else's.

"Show yourself!" Umberto spoke up, channeling one of

his tough guy parts and tensing the muscles of his neck. The star attempted to puff himself up like a snake, but only made himself redder in the face.

There was a high pitched squeal as the shadow jumped out onto the path, knocking Umberto to his ass with an unmanly flop.

She could see it now in the light. It was a large pig, a boar. It paused for a moment, sizing up the group with beady black eyes and white curled tusks before darting into the jungle behind a prone Umberto.

There was a moment of stunned silence before Tito ruined it.

"Why did you let it escape?" he asked Umberto.

"Che?" Umberto flicked a dirt clod off his golden mustache.

"We could have chopped it up and used it for set dressing!"

The old man laughed, looking around at the rest of the crew trying to get them to join in on the joke. Jacque didn't bother translating it for the English speakers. He just knelt and picked up his bag. Daria agreed that it was too hot for jokes.

After ten more minutes of walking, they found the village.

Chapter 5
Denny

The first time Dennis Roth got high on something other than liquor was in a movie theater on 42nd Street. It wasn't one of The Deuce's many porno theaters, but they catered to the same clientele, so it might as well have been. The crowd was comprised of people too poor, drunk or stoned to make a fuss about the smell of the place, or the occasional warm spots you found clinging to your seat.

That night two years ago, Denny sat in this musty theater and was so broke that he was savoring each individual Jujyfruit, trying to get them to last through the entire double bill.

When the first feature had ended—a movie called *Up from the Depths* which was exactly like *Jaws*, only minus the artistic worth or entertainment value—he got up to stretch his legs and go to the john. Going to the bathroom was a tricky proposition in a place like this, and he was on his guard.

He tensed up when the girl approached him, bouncing the baggy against her palm. Suspicious, it took Denny a while to make sure she wasn't packing either a gun or a dick. She was dynamite though, so when she asked him if he wanted to get high there wasn't much debate. The girl was all legs and spandex and bad ideas.

The next thing he knew, she was tying him off with her teeth. He was over the moon. They held hands for a bit and then fell asleep during the second movie. It had been a softcore Tito Bronze vampire flick by the name of *Blood Delight* (the domestic title) and it was the best movie-going experience of Dennis' young life.

It was now a couple of years later and the girl from the theater was long gone, but the smack habit had stuck around. Denny wasn't watching Tito Bronze movies anymore. He was making them.

He was making them *damn well.* Denny's steady hand and ability to stretch a dollar were Tito's real secret to success. Tito needed him because there were no dollies, cranes or helicopters, not within a hundred miles of a Bronze production. Denny's skills ensured that even when the plots didn't make any sense and the scheduling was tight: shit was in focus, framed properly and carried depth-of-field that was fucking *deep.*

If anything, the heroin had made him better at his job. The junk turned him skinny, caused him to itch like his forearms were made of mosquito bites, and left a terrible taste in his mouth whenever he nodded off. But the smack also opened up a kind of third eye for the "chin-e-ma," as Tito would say.

The hippies dropped acid to create their whacked-out shit, and Denny shot horse to make his blood and beaver pictures.

All of that was fine and good, but he was also getting less and less time between fixes. This increased need became a problem in situations like this one they had brewing here on the island: close quarters situations where he was forced to be around people for an extended period of time.

Upon walking out of the dense jungle and entering the village, the urge was ripping through Denny like a hungry earthworm burrowing through the veins in his arm. Sweat dripped between his shoulder blades and his hands shook as he bounded through the jungle, ducking under branches and stopping in his tracks every so often to listen for voices in the distance.

Earlier, as they walked through the huts and looked for signs of life, he was hurting so bad that he didn't really give a shit that the village was deserted. Now that he was alone with his thoughts, he allowed himself a sliver of concern that the abandoned town meant that they weren't making a movie. That was beyond his control. At least now he was getting some alone time with his needle and spoon.

"This may seem like a bad time," he had said back in the village, picking up a piece of dusty pottery. "But I really have to take a shit." He let the terracotta bowl slip from his hand and it crashed to the ground in a puff of red dust. The sound reverberated out into the empty collection of native housing.

"I don't think they big on toilet paper here," Tito said. "Or indoor plumbing."

"Banana leaves," Jacque said with a shit-fondling smile on his face. He knew full well what Denny was going to do out in the jungle. The mouthy jig was torturing him. *Why did I think that? Jacque is a nice guy.* The need always made him edgy.

"I won't go too far, and I'll keep an eye out for any villagers or whatever." Denny's words were as put-together as he could make them while all the pores of his face were opening up and screaming for a fix. He ducked into the tall grass surrounding the village and headed south.

It was as if somebody hit the light switch as he crossed into the jungle. In the village, the sun was waning; but under the dense canopy of the jungle, nighttime was in full swing. Trying his best to remember landmarks, Denny walked south until it was impossible to hear the chatter of the rest as they searched the village.

"Fuck you, pig," Denny found himself muttering every time he heard a twig snap somewhere in the darkening forest around him. When he deemed he was far enough into the wild, he stopped and wedged his ass between the intersecting trunks of two overlapping trees. The boughs made a cozy little seat, perfect for sitting down and cooking a fix.

He tried to whistle as he opened his kit, but the complete silence enveloping him as he puckered his lips kept him quiet. His hands shook as he tried to untie his balloon of golden magic powder.

"What are you doing?" a voice asked from the darkness.

Denny jumped, juggling the balloon between his sweaty fingers before clasping a tight fist around his valuables.

"Who's there?" Denny froze and began to stammer. "This isn't what it looks like." He scrambled for something that could provide some semblance of an excuse. "I…I'm a diabetic."

The little black woman stepped out of the darkness, stooped and gnarled by time.

"Oh thank god," Denny said, not only relieved that he wasn't caught by someone on the crew, but also to see a 'native' at long last. "Hello, ma'am," he said, giving her a short Miss America wave and peering into the darkness. "My name is Dennis Roth. I'm with the movie." He kept his voice loud and slow, figuring that she probably couldn't speak English. *But didn't she ask what he was doing?*

The old woman took a step forward, leaning on a curved driftwood cane for support. Her eyes were glassy black pearls, stuck far back in her head and surrounded by sunken brown skin. She blinked once.

"The film. *Pelicula. Cinoche.*" Denny held his hands up to his face and pretended to crank a camera.

"You're making a film on our island?" The old woman's voice was soft and warm and it swabbed each of his ears like a velvet Q-tip. There was something both pleasant and strange about the sensation.

"Where are the rest of you?" Denny asked her and

squinted into the rapidly darkening jungle. He needed to discern whether his new friend was alone. There was no movement behind her. The only sound in the dusk was the rattle of her jewelry as she stepped forward once again.

Her hair was weaved with seashells. More bits of shell and polished coral hung around her neck in long ropes. The ropes were longer than traditional necklaces. They were more like primitive versions of his grandmother's rosaries.

"What's wrong with your feet?" Denny asked. This close to the old woman, he could see that her feet were on backwards, the heels facing him. It wasn't ghastly. They weren't twisted or broken. They just faced the wrong way.

"Never you mind that. It doesn't matter," she said, and Denny felt that she was right: it didn't matter. "You don't need what's in that case, boy." She motioned to the small black bag in his hand: his fix kit. His stash, *man*.

Before he had a chance to think about what she meant by that, he realized what was so special about the old woman. She wasn't speaking English, but he could understand her anyway. These Euro directors like Tito, even some of the bigger boys like Leone: they were all too cheap to roll live sound on their films. All their movies had the dialogue track recorded separately. Even when it was the same language, the dubbing never matched up properly.

The old woman's lips reminded him of that. They were moving in wide foreign circles, her tough clicking down occasionally against her dirty teeth, but her words were reaching his ears in English.

"You're hearing what you want to hear, Denny," she said. He didn't question how she was doing this, how she knew his name, how she knew what he was thinking. All he wanted to do was listen to her.

"Hand that over here, child." She had gotten closer to

him than he had realized. Holding out one hand, she unfurled her long skinny fingers and gave them a slight flutter. Denny placed his kit in her small hand.

"Who are you?" was what Denny wanted to say, but somehow the words came out: "Who am I?"

"You're one of us, Dennis. You are not like the rest of those people in your group."

"Yeah, you're right," Denny said, feeling a bit more lucid now. Her words were giving him power. It felt good.

The old woman ran a small pink tongue over her brown lips before speaking again. "Listen carefully now, child. What you need to do is this."

The nearby crack of the gunshot smacked Denny in the ears. There was a dropping feeling in his stomach as the sound crashed him back down into the jungle. Denny crunched his eyes shut against the shock.

When he opened them, the old woman was gone.

"What the hell was that?" he spoke to himself, prying his butt out of the crook of the tree. He ran back toward the village, not sure whether he was high or not, and wondering where his stash kit had gone.

Chapter 6
Jacque

The boar was dead in one shot, but its body didn't seem to get the message. It squealed, blood pouring from the hole in its head, and plowed into the front of one of the huts.

The beast caught the thatched branches and dried grass of the flimsy wall with one of its tusks, and ended its life by ripping down a big chunk of island real estate with its death throes. The hut folded in upon itself in a cloud of dirt, collapsing on top of the pig.

"Fucking thing. Why would it walk into the middle of town like that?" Tito said. "Stupid, that's why." He smiled and pointed the muzzle of the small pistol to his own head, flashing the polished steel at Jacque.

"A Korovin, Soviet gun." Tito said in Spanish. "When I was just a boy, my father killed a fascist with this gun. Decades later and it's still killing pigs." That little tidbit was meant only for Jacque. Neither of the girls spoke Spanish.

Umberto had been closest to the hut when it buckled. He flicked his cigarette into the abandoned dirt road and climbed over the debris to reach the dying animal.

Daria covered her mouth, Cynthia covered her eyes and Jacque made an unsuccessful attempt not to watch as the boar twitched under the heel of Umberto's boot. Watching his step, Tito walked over the pig and gave Umberto a nod of thanks. He fired again, the gun pressed to the animal's ear. The gun smoke curled off into an elongated question mark and the pig was still, no more rattling spasms.

"Maybe it walked through town because it thought it was safe. Because nobody lives here any more and hasn't for a long time," Jacque said after a moment of silence, either from shock or out of deference for the pig. "This place is empty. Just take a look around you!"

"I do look around. All I see is civilization." Tito craned his neck in deliberate circles. "You make up stories because that's why you get paid the big money: your imagination."

Umberto shifted his weight off the corpse, finally sure that it wasn't getting back up.

"Cover it up," Tito continued, issuing orders to the actor like a sergeant to a private. "There's got to be an axe or something in one of these savage's houses. We'll cut it up before dawn, before it can rot."

Tito tucked the gun back inside his dirty suit jacket. Who would have guessed that Tito had been packing? Jacque knew what someone carrying a gun looked like, knew what to look for, but the discreet pistol fit into Tito's blazer perfectly so there was no real bulge.

There was an eruption of noise from the tall grass that bordered the tight assemblage of huts. Everyone whirled to look. Tito had the gun back out in a flash and pointed towards the rustling. *He's getting too comfortable with it,* Jacque thought.

"Shit!" Denny's familiar shrill voice rang out as he tumbled through the grass. The kid must not have been used to razor grass, and was sucking a cut on his thumb as he barreled into the open. He looked from his wound to see Tito pointing the gun at his chest.

His slim frame, scuzzy peach-fuzz and pockmarked face always made Jacque think of Denny as the kid, but really he was only a few years younger than himself. His frightened eyes made him look even younger. His fear softened into a grin as he raised both hands above his head.

"You miss all the excitement," Tito said. Denny looked at the blood running down his arm and popped the finger back in his mouth. Tito returned his weapon to his jacket. Jacque wondered what else he had in there. What further surprises could Tito possibly pack into this trip?

"Mr. Bronze killed a boar. Shot it," Cynthia said, filling Denny in. "He says he wants it for special effects. Blood and stuff." She then turned to Jacque and whispered: "Do you think I will have to touch it?"

"He'll want you to bathe in it," Jacque said, watching her toffee cheeks go flush with squeamish terror and embarrassment. "But don't worry: I will write around it, make it so that only who-ever is playing the cannibals will ever have to touch it."

Cynthia smiled, swiping the end of her nose with a finger like the con-men in *The Sting*. He returned the gesture, becoming the Redford to her Newman.

"That's assuming that we ever shoot a frame of film."

He looked up at the sky. Stars were becoming visible. The number and intensity of stars was amazing. Even in the British countryside, he'd never seen so many. They were beautiful.

"Maybe the villagers are on a trip and will be back in the morning," Denny said. "Either way, we've got to shoot. We should make camp and get some sleep so we don't waste any daylight. I'm beat."

"Agreed," Tito said, and then translated the plan into Italian for the rest of the crew. "Someone should go gather wood for a fire," he added in French, meaning that Jacque was the intended 'someone.'

"Don't worry, old man. You've had a long day. I'll go look for firewood," Jacque responded in English. Tito frowned.

It was no secret that Jacque was trying to stir up insurrection among the English-speaking members of the crew.

"I'll go with you, could be dangerous," Cynthia said. In the moonlight he could see that above her dimples were the tiniest of caramel-colored freckles. Maybe this wouldn't be the worst shoot of Jacque's career after all.

Chapter 7
Cynthia

"I should have corrected what Mr. Bronze said on the plane before. I'm not a mulatto," she said, angling the flashlight up to Jacque's face so she could gauge his reaction.

"Oh?" He sounded like he was unsure whether there was a joke coming or not.

"I'm actually a *quadroon*. My mother was a halfie," she said with mock fright, pointing the flashlight up to her face, as if she'd just reached the punchline of a scary story. "My hair really is this straight. So I'm not trying to 'look white' or anything like that, if things like that are sensitive issues for you."

"Don't worry, Sister," Jacque held up a 'right on' fist and smiled. "I don't really go in for all that stuff. I only take offense when someone is being an asshole."

She giggled.

"I didn't mean to swear," he said, looking down at his shoes, and then bent to pick up a twig that wasn't even big enough to categorize as kindling, adding it to the bundle under his arm. This guy, this multilingual Cambridge graduate, was nervous being around her. It made her feel special, but not entirely comfortable.

"Don't apologize." She wanted to put him at ease. Men tripped over themselves every time she stepped foot on the island of Manhattan, from Harlem to The Village. Normally she welcomed it, but on *this* island getaway, she wanted a vacation from all that crap. "Looking at the men on this trip, I have a feeling that I'm going to hear a lot worse than 'asshole' over the next three days. For the first time in my life, I'm thankful that the only languages I speak are English and the bits of Yiddish I've picked up at the deli."

"Which reminds me," he said with a surge of confidence in his voice. "You shouldn't call Tito Mr. Bronze. It makes him sound like he deserves a modicum of respect. He doesn't."

"I figured as much," she said. The darkness surrounding them was close to total, so even with the flashlight they'd unpacked, the pair stayed close to camp. "Where do you think everyone is?" she asked while handing him a larger stick.

"I don't think there is an 'everyone'," he said and sighed like a doctor giving a patient some very bad news. "I think Tito looked at a map or maybe an out-of-date almanac, pointed to a destination that looked small, and didn't even bother to check if it was still inhabited."

"Well, there were people here at one point," she said, ducking to pick up a dead, fallen branch. "Where did they all go?"

"There were fishing nets in all of the huts, but only a few boats. Maybe there was a change in season and they followed the fish to a different island."

"You don't sound like you believe that." She pointed the thick branch at his chest, bits of lichen flaking off in her hand and turning to dust on his lapel.

"No, probably because I don't," he said, his voice serious now. "The town is deserted and has been for a while. Nobody packed up their belongings, they just left. They wouldn't have left their homes behind. Maybe they were evacuated for a nuclear test? I know the U.S. couldn't get enough of that kind of thing in the 50s and 60s."

"That makes me feel better," she laughed and socked him in the arm with the branch.

There was something wrong with the hit, and Jacque sensed it, too. The branch had no give. It didn't bend, it didn't break: it just molted a bit more, revealing a smooth white interior.

It wasn't a branch at all. It was a bone.

A human femur.

Jacque yelped before Cynthia had the chance to do so herself. She loosened her kung-fu grip on the bone, and it fell to the forest floor with a soft thud.

The "bark" had been mummified flesh, twisting off in her hand and shedding into dust as she flailed the goddamn thing around. She put her hand up to her face; it was stained with brownish-red dust, and smelled like mildew.

Jacque took her by the filthy hand. He was either not aware of what he was grabbing hold of, or he didn't care. She wanted the touch, too.

Cynthia pointed the flashlight beam to the ground and they both screamed again as they realized what they were standing on. Not a burial ground, but a dumping ground.

They were knee-deep in corpses, maybe two dozen of them.

The bodies beyond the beam were easy to spot in the moonlight. Exposed glints of off-white bone shone in the night where flesh formerly clung. Elbows, knees and the occasional ribcage poked up from the moist ground. If these bodies had once been buried, then their grave hadn't been very deep or very private.

There was an excited stirring in the camp as the rest of the crew ran out to meet them, their calls for direction echoing in the darkness.

Tito was the first to arrive. *Where did this fat little old creep find the energy?*

"Looks like we finally found the natives," he said. "This is great. Amazing on-screen value."

Cynthia didn't raise the flashlight to look at his crooked yellow smile, but she knew it was there.

Chapter 8
Umberto

The rest of them were asleep. After the bleach-blonde with the dark skin had calmed down about the skeletons, the crew had dusted off five thatched bedrolls and camped in the two huts adjacent to the small fire Umberto had started.

Umberto would have been asleep, too, if he hadn't taken a handful of uppers to balance himself out this afternoon as they disembarked the plane. Like the rest of them, he had been expecting to work. He hadn't planned on a day-long hike along the beach and then through the jungle. Being the internationally renowned gentleman he was, Umberto also had to tow the heaviest piece of luggage along with him.

His palms were sore as he sat brooding in front of the fire. The drugs still caused his heart to pound against his chest, making it impossible to sleep no matter how much he wanted to.

Umberto had always loved fire, and now he held his fingers as close as he could to the flames. It was a game he played as a child: seeing how long he could take the heat. The soot from the fire turned the tips of his fingers black.

He sat on his hands, warming his ass cheeks and staring off into the night.

The jungle beyond the camp was silent except for the constant hum of crickets and something that sounded like cicadas; did they have cicadas in the middle of the ocean? Umberto usually disliked quiet. He was a man of action and stillness didn't calm him.

But sitting by the fire and listening to the bugs was—he had to admit—enjoyable. Possibly because he didn't have to listen to the rest of the crew jabbering to each other in eighty different fucking languages, only snatches of which he could understand.

A gust of wind batted and bent the tall grass behind the fire. The wind brought with it the fresh smell of the sea, and a gentle howl.

Under any other circumstances, on any other island, this would have been a great night. For example, if they had decided to film in Rio, he would have found himself two card games and a whore by now. Even better, if they were in Southern Italy, he wouldn't have to bother with finding the whore: he was a semi-familiar face back home, and ladies love a celebrity.

Here on this dead, unnamed island, he was forced to sit quite literally with his thumb up his ass. It didn't make the situation much better that his thumb was warm.

He swiveled and looked at the burlap door that led to the hut behind him. Inside that hut, he guessed that the two girls were curled up, probably hugging each other for warmth and safety. Umberto could provide them with both protection and companionship.

He smiled at the thought and tugged at his crotch. His hands were still pleasantly warm. Maybe he should slip in there and try to snuggle up next to the makeup girl with the big breasts and the alright face, or maybe the cute little cube of brown sugar with the blonde hair.

He thought of the moolie writer in the next hut, and his smile dissolved into a frown. Old Jacque would probably have a problem if he tried to move in on his woman. Umberto didn't have any real problem with moolies, but he fucking hated frogs.

Stuck up foreign *puttanas*, not giving him the time of day, who did they think they were? A beauty school dropout and some halfie from the States, that's what Tito had told him. How is it possible that Umberto was not making it with one of them right now? At least one of them!

He turned back around and gazed out into the tall grass again. There was a form staring back at him now.

Stumbling, he tried to jump to his feet.

"Don't be afraid," the shape said. Its eyes were perfectly framed by the thick grass that hid everything else from view.

"Who are you?" Umberto asked, curious how any Caribbean islander had learned Italian.

The person in the grass shushed him. "You'll wake the others. Come over here so we can talk without you shouting."

It didn't seem like a great idea to Umberto, and it wasn't his machismo pride that made him listen to the mysterious stranger, but the stranger's voice itself. Umberto could not tell whether it was a man or a woman's voice; but either way, it ebbed and flowed its way into his mind, telling him everything was alright with just its intonation.

Before he even noticed his legs were moving, Umberto was putting up his hands to push the tall grass away from his face.

"What Umberto Luigi wants more than anything is the role of a lifetime," the shape said. He couldn't tell what it was in the moonlight.

"What are you?" It was both male and female, tall and short, black and white, old and young. Just when Umberto thought he could comprehended a stable image of it, he would catch the glint of an eye as it changed color or the wisp of a beard where he thought there had been a smooth-shaven cheek.

"I can give you what you want, Umberto. I can give you the role that will make you known all over the world." The figure ignored his question, and he began to forget that he had even asked one to begin with. The shape's offer echoed in his head.

"What would I have to do?" he asked.

The shape smiled, first as an old black woman, then as a tall bearded white man glistening with sweat and grime. "To begin, go back to the village and get a blade."

As the words came, so did pictures. Umberto saw in his mind's eye where the machete was kept. "Then you must quietly take the boar into the jungle."

Umberto smiled. His dream role lay out before him and all he had to do was grab it. "I think I know exactly what the third step is," he said, turning his back on the shape and heading back through the grass.

He was very quiet as he uncovered the boar. Its hair was coarse and wiry on his neck as he slung the beast over his shoulder and disappeared into the forest. The machete dangled from his belt, gleaming in the starlight.

Chapter 9
Denny

The thin bedroll was as hard and unforgiving as the ground under it, but it only took a few moments for Denny to pass into a heavy sleep.

He awoke several times to noises in the night, the picture of a stooped old black woman still fresh in his mind and foreign whispers in his ears. These moments were brief, and after each he would dive back into unconsciousness with minimal effort.

The first blades of morning light cut through the window of the hut, and he awoke for good.

As Denny crawled under the doorway, he didn't feel rested. He felt sore and sweaty, and there was the strange tickle of a headache at the base of his neck. *Maybe I did miss a fix yesterday*, he thought before realizing that if chemical withdrawal were indeed setting in, it would have been a shitload worse than this.

The dry mouth was pretty bad, though. His tongue felt like crêpe paper as he ran it over his mossy teeth, and it stuck like glue. Before touching the equipment to set up for the morning's shots, he wandered to the east end of town and stopped at the well that Jacque had found last night.

The well wasn't made of mortar and stone, neither did it have a little gazebo on top like all the wells that Denny had ever seen in the movies. This well was just a three foot hole in the ground covered with three slats of wood and a basket on a rope.

He lowered the basket down and up, his elbows aching from the effort. The water was brown and musty, but cold enough that he was tempted to gulp it right down. Last night, Jacque had made a big show of finding a shallow metal dish in one of the huts and boiling their water. Jacque may have been an intelligent guy, but he was also a pussy.

"Drink," a voice said at the back of his mind. If he boiled it, it wouldn't have felt as nice as it did coursing down his throat.

After drinking his fill, Denny splashed the rest on his neck and chest, his morning shower probably covering him with more dirt than he'd started with.

Inside of the hut, he could still hear Tito snoring. That was good. He didn't need the old man hassling him while he loaded the camera and unpacked the rest of the equipment.

Tito was a pain, but boy could the man talk. Last night, it had taken the director less than an hour to defuse the situation with the dead bodies. He had convinced the writer and the actress that he sympathized with their point, and was just as disturbed as they were to find a mass grave, but the plane wasn't coming back for another two days so they might as well make the movie a testament to the islander's lives.

Denny didn't buy that testament bit, and he was sure that the rest of them didn't either. But they had nowhere to go, and a movie to make.

It took half an hour of putting everything in order before Denny was stricken with abject panic.

Where is my meter? A cameraman's light meter is only slightly less important to him than his pecker. Denny clawed through the excelsior of the big crate, tossing clumps out onto the ground until he was certain that the crate was empty.

"Look at this mess," Tito said from behind him. "What are you doing?" The old man stretched in the dawn. Tito wore only his shorts and his suit jacket. He didn't look at Denny, but instead picked specks of sand from his chest hair.

"Looking for my light meter," Denny said.

"It's around your neck."

Denny's fear abated, but it didn't make him feel much better. He clutched at the gadget, slapping it against his chest.

"I was going to get some coverage of the huts, maybe some inserts of bare feet in the sand," Denny said.

"Are you calling the shots now?" Tito gave a blank stare back, if it was possible to rub one's belly in an intimidating manner, than the old man was doing so.

"No, I'm sorry. What do you want to start with? Mein director?"

"Coverage sounds good," Tito said and let his hands fall slack. "Everyone wake up! You're all late to set! I'm docking your pay," he yelled to the huts, his voice sending a flock of birds out of the trees and up into the early morning sky.

The others began to stumble into the open and Tito got up close to Denny. "I like you, Denny. You're great at what you do," Tito said, his voice a whisper. "But don't you ever fucking shoot a single frame of film without my say-so."

Tito slapped him on the shoulder and Denny nodded, feeling like a disciplined preschooler.

After taking some light readings and messing with the aperture, Denny stood in front of the camera and outstretched both his hands, parting the small crowd Moses-style. Jacque shuttled the girls out of the way of the camera and Tito took a few steps over. Denny ducked out from behind the set-up and then remembered that the Golden Guinea was not among them.

"Jacque, could you please go back into the hut and wake up Umberto so he doesn't wander through the shot?"

"He wasn't in there with us," Jacque said, motioning to the tent. It figured that the brainiac would double up with the women. Jacque had all the luck.

"Well he wasn't with us last night," Tito said. "Probably passed out by the fire."

"Then where is he now?" Jacque asked.

Alright, Perry Mason, enough with the questions. I want to shoot, Denny thought. He felt a single bead of sweat glide over the hair above his ass cheeks. It was early and the sun was on the move. If he didn't shoot now, he would miss the soft light of dawn.

"Probably taking a shit. What do I know? He ate the tuna on the plane, big mistake," Tito said. "Just get out of Denny's way."

"Finally!" Denny got into position behind the set-up, unlocked the x-axis on the tripod, tightened up the tilt and gripped the pan handle. He then pressed his eye tight to the viewfinder, blocking out any light that could seep in and prematurely expose the film.

"Whatever happens today, don't you dare cut the camera, child," a familiar voice said into his ear.

"What was that?" Denny turned to look at Tito.

"I say nothing."

He shrugged and inhaled deep, holding his breath as he started rolling. There was the familiar mechanical whir and in a few moments of flawless movement it was over.

It was a beautiful, smooth pan. Ten seconds of the movie was now shot, twenty when Tito used the footage twice.

Chapter 10
Cynthia

Cynthia watched Jacque carefully as he spoke to Tito. There was an uneasiness in both men, as if they were both braced for a fight. It wasn't openly hostile, and it wasn't devoid of familiarity, but there was violence to it nonetheless. "Okay writer. We got three people, two women and a man and no natives. Which scene should we start with?" Tito asked.

"Right now we don't even have Umberto. We've only got Cynthia. I don't have any scenes with just her in an empty village…or just her alone in the jungle for that matter. We need at least Umberto."

"Sweetheart," Tito said, snapping his fingers at the makeup girl, Daria. He said something to her in Italian. She nodded and smiled before saying: "No English."

"No English," Tito mimicked back and smiled. "She won't need English. There we go, we've got two actresses. I bet this little peach will take her top off, too." Tito indicated the makeup girl who was still smiling, no idea what he was saying. "Add them to our newest leading man," the old man drilled a finger into Jacque's chest, "and you've got a movie."

"No," Jacque said. No humor or familiarity, just flat refusal.

"Yes. Look around. You see any cannibals? You see any-one who can even pass for a cannibal?" Tito asked. His impish smile looked to Cynthia like his body smelled: ripe with decay. Every time you thought he couldn't get any slimier, he said something even more odious. The man was a pig and a bigot.

The thought of a pig made Cynthia's eyes wander to the wrecked hut and the dead boar, but the body was gone.

"I direct," Tito continued, raising his voice and snapping her attention away from the missing swine. "Denny works the camera. What is it that you do, Jacque? It looks to me like you eat pretty girls for dinner."

Cynthia noticed Tito wasn't dropping articles of speech anymore. The demented little old man's English was as strong as he wanted it to be in any given situation. Jacque was right: the man was a huckster, but a good one.

"You can't make me do anything," Jacque said.

"You're right," Tito said, patting his suit jacket pocket. *Did he just touch his gun on purpose?*

"Are you threatening me?" Jacque didn't miss the implication either.

"Only with the fact that if you don't help, there will be no movie," Tito dipped into his pocket and pulled out a cigarette. "And no paycheck. Actors get paid more. You do know that, right? And of course, you'd still be receiving your writing credit."

"Because I'm working with you for the valuable screen credit," Jacque said under his breath. "Fine. Let's do it."

Tito spoke something in Italian to Daria, who responded: "Momento" and walked over to the biggest crate. She picked out some of the long strands of wood wool they had used as packing material, and then fished around in her makeup kit.

Approaching Jacque, she spoke in Italian, sounding embarrassed. He laughed and said something back that caused her to go red in the face.

Jacque began to unbutton his shirt. "She's going to paint me so I look like one of Tito's 'savages,'" he said to Cynthia.

"You don't have to do this," Cynthia said.

Jacque folded his shirt and handed it to her. His muscles weren't huge, but they were well-defined, and his unblemished dark skin glistened in the sun. A shirtless Jacque was not an unpleasant sight. She would go to see this movie.

Daria approached him with a paintbrush and then lowered it. She said something else that Cynthia couldn't understand and reached for his belt, starting to undo it before he intervened.

Jacque laughed. "Don't worry. I've got it," he said in English for Cynthia's benefit, pushing Daria's hand away. Daria shrugged and went at him with the paint brush.

The Italian girl drew brilliant pastel green lines down his chest and arms, then switched to a smaller brush and did some detail work in bright red.

"I look like I belong to the same tribe as Santa Claus," he said. It was true: he looked ridiculous and not the least bit scary.

After considering how she could improve the situation for a moment, Cynthia approached one of the huts and tore off a bit of tree bark. The bark was light and spongy, covered in green bits of lichen, and was used as roofing shingles by the locals. She punched two eyeholes with her thumbs and tied a string of the packing material to both sides.

"Here put this on, you can hide your face and stay in good standing with the NAACP," Cynthia said, handing him the impromptu tribal mask. "Plus, it looks better."

Tito nodded his approval and Jacque slipped on the mask.

"We should get all we can while we have the camera already set up. Can you think of a scene that would involve the two of you in the village?" Denny asked Jacque, then glanced back at Tito.

"Don't forget to include the makeup girl," Tito said.

"Naked."

"Well, Cynthia plays a photojournalist who is investigating a series of disappearances on a resort beach. In the beginning of the film, she learns that a primitive tribe is boating over from a nearby island—thought deserted—and they're abducting pretty young tourist girls. She travels to the island with the help of her dashing and handsome guide, Umberto's character," Jacque said, his voice self-serious before catching himself: "Honestly, it's an absolute classic."

Tito shaded his eyes with one hand and looked up at the sun. "And? The scene right now?"

"Well, you can have Daria here play one of the abducted tourists. The cannibal I play can be bringing her back to camp and begin making dinner preparations while the rest of the tribe is off in the jungle chasing Umberto's character," Jacque said as Daria tucked handfuls of the packing material into the waistband of his underwear, transforming it into a passable grass skirt. "Cynthia's character can be following us, snapping pictures and looking for a way to free Daria."

"Perfect. One more thing, though," Tito said. He went down on one knee in front of the fire pit. The motion was so alien to his bulky frame that the old man looked like he was going to topple over into the mud.

After sifting through the last few embers of the fire, Tito spit into his palms and rubbed the ash over his hands. Rising, he came up behind Daria and began smudging her face with deep black marks from the ash and dirt. The girl recoiled and screeched in Italian. Tito just laughed and apologized.

"Scusi. Mi scusi…"

Cynthia didn't know anything about Italian intonation, but he didn't sound sincere.

Turning to the rest of the crew, Tito made a big show that he was entering director mode. He rubbed his temples, framed shots with his fingers, and barked out blocking decisions and marks to the actors, all while chain smoking and switching between three languages. His theatrics may have looked self-indulgent, but so were the motions of most famous composers, and they were still respected.

When he was finished, Cynthia had a strong grip on the geography of the set-up, what she and the rest of the cast were supposed to be doing and when. Why were the assholes always so talented?

Chapter 11
Denny

"Action," Tito screamed from somewhere beyond.

The director's voice was in another world from the one Denny allowed himself to inhabit. Tito was in the world outside the frame. Tito had made the decision to let Denny go handheld for the shot. It would be a greater strain on the actors, but would allow them to shoot more footage more quickly if they could pull it off in one take.

The movie they were ripping off, *Cannibal Fury Atrocity* or whatever it was called, had been shot in the style of a faux-documentary. Both Jacque and Tito had agreed that they would take a more traditional approach to the subject matter, but a few extended shots with the camera resting on Denny's shoulder wouldn't hurt them.

Denny had been so high when he first saw *Halloween* last year that the film's point-of-view shots had wheedled their way into his subconscious and kept him awake for three days straight (well, it was either John Carpenter or the speed). He wanted to use the camera in his arms to replicate that feeling right now.

He was feeling strong and sharp: no Steadicam, no problem. Maybe if he pulled this off they could even restructure the film so that this could be the opening sequence.

Through the viewfinder, in front of the jungle landscape, he watched his own name materialize in the credits. Director of

Photography Dennis Roth. *No, no time for daydreams of glory. Time to work*, he told himself.

Tito had suggested that they begin the shot out in the jungle, with Denny and the camera following Jacque, who had the makeup girl slung over one shoulder, and then dropping back to reveal that Cynthia's photojournalist was following both of them and snapping pictures. When they reached the tall grass, Denny crouched low so that the camera lens was right up against the stalks, pushing the grass out of the way with the lens as he inched forward.

"Now! *Destare*," Tito yelled from a few yards behind the camera. He was telling the makeup girl to wake up as they entered the clearing before the village. The shot had begun with Daria unconscious, remaining motionless while carried by Jacque. She lifted her smudged face to the camera, remaining careful not to make eye contact with the lens and beating against Jacque's back with her fist. Good.

Her hits were actually connecting and Denny could hear the wet smack and see the ripples in his flesh as Jacque strained his muscles to hold her up. It was a shame that they weren't rolling sound, because that sound effect would be impossible to recreate on a soundstage. It was beautiful. Even if they botched the rest of the take, they could use this footage.

Denny slowed his steps, allowing Jacque to pull away from the camera as they entered the village. Trying to keep his breaths steady, Denny exhaled and panned the camera over to reveal Cynthia sneaking out of the tall grass.

"Take a picture, darling," Tito said and the actress leveled her prop camera to her eye and clicked the shutter.

Finding her and putting her on screen may end up being Tito Bronze's only lasting contribution to cinema. She was beautiful and the camera loved her. Denny could feel the pure power of her exotic presence as the sound of the frames whirring by pressed against his ear. The camera was heavy. His body was covered in sweat but he didn't dare let a single tremor reach his hands. He would complete this shot if it killed him.

Cynthia stepped into the clearing and Denny panned again: forming a two shot with Jacque in the background and Cynthia in the fore. Ducking low to the ground, Cynthia continued toward the camp, snapping twigs and leaves. She mimed stealth but did not achieve it. Denny made sure not to catch her feet in the frame; it would ruin the illusion if you saw that she was clearly making noise.

"Scream," Tito said, but Daria couldn't understand him. Denny heard Jacque mumble something in Italian from beneath his mask, and the girl let out a yell, ropes of spittle flying from her mouth.

"Put her in front of the fire," Tito said from Denny's left side, still keeping his distance so his shadow did not enter the frame. Denny felt a sharp bubble of pain move in his stomach and heard an accompanying grumble. *Ignore it*, he told himself, and tightened his grip on the camera.

Jacque set Daria down in a puff of dirt and dust, not trying to hurt her, but not looking overly concerned with her safety either. That was good: indifference would read better on the screen.

"Now rip her top off," Tito said. Jacque's muscles immediately tensed in response; Tito had plucked at his spinal column as if it were a guitar string. "Do it now. Careful not to get her bra in the first go."

Daria looked up at her attacker. Her puzzlement at Jacque's hesitation didn't ruin the scene. It enhanced it, gave it depth of character.

Denny's stomach gave his nervous system another quick jab so painful that he almost dipped the camera. *Shit*, he thought, *I'm going to fuck all this up because I didn't boil my water*. He clenched his teeth until the roots sung against the pressure. He kept the focus steady.

Jacque finally snapped out of it, giving himself over to the part and howling under his mask that he was sorry before gripping onto Daria's blouse. The first jerk of his hand sent two large buttons flying into the fire at his feet.

Daria's screaming changed. The part was real for her now, and her surprise would pay big dividends when they reviewed the footage in the editing room. Denny realized that Tito had told his other two actors much more about the scene than he translated into Italian for the girl. He had deliberately kept her unaware of what was going to happen.

Daria fought back against Jacque, smacking his forearms with open palms before attempting to claw at his chest.

"Keep going," Denny heard himself say aloud. He would probably catch shit from Tito for directing, but it didn't matter because this was gold. A snake of pain crawled along his lower intestine, but it didn't matter. The frenzy was upon him now and he was using the thrill of sensation to keep himself in the game.

Jacque batted her hands away and hooked a finger around one bra strap. "I'm sorry," he said again as he tugged the brassiere free. Her breasts were large, with prominent tan lines drawn across her olive flesh that left her nipples pleasantly pale. The camera loved them almost as much as it loved Cynthia's face.

Denny did a quick rack focus to make Cynthia's expression crystal clear. Repulsion and fear were etched across her pretty face. The emotions were authentic. Denny doubted that she was that good an actor.

Denny opened up the focus to bring the whole grotesque tableau into an even clarity. Tito would yell cut soon, but Denny didn't want to stop.

Denny nearly dropped the camera when he caught a glimpse of Umberto walking out of the jungle between the two huts in the background. *He'll ruin everything!*

"What is he doing!" Tito said. His voice equally dismayed by their star's appearance.

Jacque turned to look at the golden haired Italian. Denny wondered when he had time to get into makeup and costume, before realizing that Umberto wasn't supposed to be playing a savage.

Denny had heard stories of crazy actors, but Umberto's stunt was less Klaus Kinski, more Charlie Manson. *What the fuck is he wearing?*

As the actor stepped into focus, he got his answer.

He was wearing nothing but the pig.

Umberto's entire body was slippery and red. He wore a dripping fur loincloth around his waist, held the machete in one hand. The crazy bastard had severed the top of the boar's skull at the mouth and wore it over his blonde hair like a hat, letting the rest of the pelt flow behind him like a gore-strewn cape.

"Bellissimo," Tito yelled. "Such production value."

Daria was the only one among them who had not seen him yet. Umberto stepped over the fire, not flinching as he passed through the flames.

"What are you doing?" Jacque asked. In response, Umberto shouldered him out of the way and grabbed a clump of Daria's hair.

"Remember. Whatever you do: don't cut the camera," the old woman's voice whispered to Denny.

He didn't.

He caught it all.

Chapter 12
Daria

Daria felt a single tear trickle down her cheek. She hated that she was crying for these bastards. These were pigs that would hire a girl under false pretenses. They brought her thousands of miles away from home to brutalize her for their shitty movie.

This was probably what Bronze had in mind from the second she stepped into his office, and he couldn't take his eyes off her tits. The black one seemed nice, but in the end he was just the same as the others.

More tears came as her head was jerked back.

The smell of Umberto hit her before the sight of him did. He smelled sweet and salty, like candied meat.

His face was not nearly as ambiguous. Veins pulsed in his neck and forehead; rivulets of partially congealed blood dripped from the snout of the pig at the top of his head. His maniac smile was framed at the top by his blonde mustache, now dyed red with pig blood and matted at the corners with whitish-pink froth.

She tore her eyes away from his and they landed on the blade in his hand. It was no prop. They had not brought that with them off the plane.

"This has gone too far," she screamed, thinking that at least Umberto would be able to understand her. He didn't react, and her attention remained glued to the long, blood-flecked knife.

On her second official makeup assignment for school, back when she could afford school, Daria was working with a woman who told her that she used to be an actress. The woman was only a few years older than Daria herself, so Daria had asked why she'd chosen to retire so early.

The woman gave her a warm smile and laughed. "I didn't choose to retire," she said. As Daria curled her lashes and experimented with different shades of eyes shadow, the woman told her the story.

"When I was first starting out," the woman told her. "I would take any jobs that were offered to me. Anything to keep my name out there and keep bread on the table, you know? So on maybe my fifth or sixth film—a horror movie—I figured that I was an old pro." She rolled her eyes, causing Daria to smudge her work. "The thing that you start believing when you're on movie sets so often, is that everything around you is complete make-believe. So on the last night of shooting this film, it's my character's best moment. She has been cornered by the killer and must fight his weapon away from him or be killed."

By this point, Daria had forgotten all about the assignment, putting down her materials and listening to the woman's story. The cinema was the business she was destined for, and she relished first-hand accounts any chance she got.

"So in this scene," the woman continued. "I am wrestling with this actor. I was giving it my all. I always used to give it my all. So as an improvisation, because I was getting *so into it*, I grabbed on to the knife as he tried to stab at me with it. No big deal, right? Because it's got to be a fake knife: everything is make-believe. Right?

"Well, it would have been, if the jokers responsible for making this movie had any idea what they were doing. The knife was real."

Daria held her hand to her mouth.

"It wasn't a prop, and it hadn't even been dulled before the scene. Fifteen stitches. It cut through tendons and veins. I've never seen so much blood, and unless there's another war, I don't think I ever will." The woman held up her hand to Daria's face. There were two long white scars running across her palm. "So much blood that I thought I was going to die, but I didn't. The production hadn't even been insured, so I didn't even get medical compensation. Now I have to write with my left hand because I can't even hold a pen."

The woman told the story with a steely detachment, but that didn't stop Daria from crying.

"Don't cry. I didn't tell you that to make you sad," the ex-actress had said. "I told you that to let you know that this business will fuck you up if you let it."

That was the last thought that went through Daria's mind.

And then the machete blade went halfway through her neck.

Chapter 13
Jacque

The girl's head didn't come off with the first swipe. But after the third swift chop, it hit the ground and rolled into the fire.

Umberto scrambled after it, picking it up and hugging it close to his chest to extinguish the flames. The result for Jacque was a splash of warm arterial spray, accompanied closely by the odor of burnt hair.

Jacque watched the rest of Daria's body waver on its knees, nerves twitching. He vomited before it could slump down to the dirt at his feet. Barely able to rip the mask off in time, his throat stung as his stomach rolled and voided.

His gagging wrested Umberto's attention away from the smoldering face he held wedged under his arm like a football.

Before he could stop himself, Jacque locked eyes with Umberto. That's exactly what you're *not* supposed to do, when dealing with a wild animal.

That's what Umberto was: a crazed animal. He wasn't a lunatic or a method actor too deep in character; he was a snarling beast, bent on mayhem, and he wasn't through yet.

"Cut! Cut *now*," Tito screamed, sounding like he was trying to will reality back into existence the only way he knew how.

Tito Bronze had directed nearly fifty films. The murders had always ended whenever he yelled cut. He was now unable to restore sanity to the situation with a simple word.

Umberto gripped Daria's scalp and tossed the head at Jacque with a quick underhand lob. Without even meaning to, as if it were some precious object that could be saved, maybe even re-attached, Jacque reached out and grabbed the head before it could hit the ground. He dropped it as soon as he felt the clammy warmth of the dead flesh.

Down in Umberto's chest, a deep rolling laugh began and he raised the machete high again. Jacque could see in his eyes that the novelty of the first murder was already beginning to wane. Umberto was ready for another.

Jacque took one look out at the rest of the crew. Cynthia was frozen in terror and disbelief. Tito had taken a step backward and was clawing at his thinning hair in frustration, still muttering 'cut.'

Denny was the only one who'd moved closer to the action, and it wasn't to help. Denny's hands were white, one clenched over the camera and the other steady on the focus ring. The eye that Jacque could see was jammed shut and the other was pressed against the viewfinder so hard that there were broken blood vessels speckling the bridge of Denny's nose.

None of them was going to be very much help.

Umberto reared back to swing and Jacque dropped out of his way, diving towards the maniac instead of away. Jacque felt the burn of the connection graze his hip before he could take the legs out from under Umberto and tackle him to the ground.

They both fell, Jacque sending his hands out in front of him. It was reflex meant to protect, but both hands landed in the dying fire. Daria's blood had mixed with the ash and dirt, forming a boiling paste that clung to Jacque's hands even after he pulled them from the flames.

Behind him, Umberto grunted and tripped over his boar fur cape in a clumsy attempt to find his footing. Umberto stead-

ied the pig skull on top of his head before trying again. Jacque
flipped himself onto his back and whipped both hands at Umberto, flinging some of the boiling sludge at his face and blinding
him.

"We're going to run out," Denny said, his voice mea-
sured, calm and professional. The young cameraman was only
a few feet away from them now, and warned the crew that they
better wrap this fight scene before he had no more unexposed
film left in the camera. This meant that Denny had lost it as well.
Given the events of the last few minutes, Jacque could hardly
blame him.

Umberto dropped the blade, screeching as he clawed at
his eyes. If the wild animal comparisons were in doubt before,
they were 100% accurate now.

Jacque pounced for the weapon, tearing his already
blistering hands as he wrapped his fingers around the hilt. He
stood, keeping the edge of the blade over Umberto's head, ready
to bring it down if the crazed Italian tried anything.

Umberto looked up at Jacque, and he could see how
badly the man was hurt. His right eye was red and inflamed,
but still open. His left was swelled shut, tears of blood streaming
from the corners. Umberto bared his teeth, lifting himself to his
feet and causing Jacque to take a step back.

"Easy," Jacque said, forgetting that Umberto couldn't
speak English. Regardless, the man seemed to get the message as
Jacque lifted the weapon higher, his grip loose around layers of
dead skin and jellied blood. If Umberto sprang, Jacque intended
on slicing through the boar snout and splitting his head down the
middle.

"Damn, we're out," Denny said and hoisted the camera
to the ground. He cradled the large piece of equipment like a
child and the viewfinder left a ring over his right eye that made
him look like the dog from the *Our Gang* shorts. "Everyone take

five while I reload."

The shock was beginning to fade, and Jacque could feel the pain radiating from his burnt hands. He sucked in air, trying to catch his breath and wondered how long he would be able to wield the machete. Jacque took a step away from Umberto and towards the rest of the group. Umberto matched it.

Jacque took another look at Tito and almost sobbed with relief. The old man had the pistol drawn and was walking towards them now. Denny picked up the camera and carried it over to the crate at the edge of town, no doubt about to use the film bag to switch in a fresh spool of 35mm.

"Oh thank God," Jacque said as Tito approached him and leveled the gun.

Umberto took another step before the gun was on him.

"Don't you move," Tito said as he pointed the gun at the maniac.

Jacque let his arms drop dead to his sides.

"Did I say you could move either, Jacque?" Inexplicably, the gun was on him now. "Nobody does anything until the boy gets more film in the camera."

Chapter 14
Cynthia

Tito pointed the gun at Jacque's gut and raised it level with his face as he spoke. Cynthia was too far away to make out the words, but the action was loud and clear. Before she could cry out in response, she saw Jacque's eyes move from the barrel of the gun to her and then back again.

He was trying to tell her something. "Run!" was the message he was trying to send her with the glance; at least she thought that's what the look meant. She hoped she had interpreted it correctly, because she dove to the ground, not needing to be told twice.

She dipped low to the dirt and ran between the two nearest huts.

"Hey, where you going?" she heard Denny call from somewhere behind her. The D.P.'s voice was despondent: he had lost it as well, but in a less violent way than the others. Always a professional, Denny was just doing his job. She ignored him and dove into the tall grass.

There was a thunderclap, and the patch of grass a foot from her face exploded as a bullet zinged by her ear. Cynthia caught a quick whiff of cordite and lawn clippings.

"That was warning shot," Tito yelled out to her. "Come back or the next one is going to be in you."

She hesitated for a moment before crouching deeper into

the cover of the grass and diving into the jungle at the other side. In the distance, she could hear curse words rendered in a myriad of languages. She ran deeper into the jungle.

Then Tito said the words she was most afraid of:

"Avanti! Go get after her!"

There were footfalls and whooping in the distance. She didn't know which direction she was running, her course altered by both her own frenzy and the twisting impediments of the jungle that she had to hop over and crawl under.

The whooping morphed into a familiar laughter. Umberto, probably once again brandishing the machete.

She had to hide or she could end up running in circles, or into the open terrain of the beach or airstrip. She would never be able to escape Umberto in a straight footrace. Even injured and half-blind, his stride was twice as long as hers.

Some kind of animal leapt between the branches above her head and caused her to look up. Even in the daylight, the tall treetops were an impenetrable tangle of overlapping leaves, vines and moss. Up was her only option.

Stifling a grunt of exertion, Cynthia shoved her hand into the nearest knot, praying there was not a snake or a bat inside. She swung her arm up to the lowest branch that looked like it would hold her weight and pulled with all her might.

There were very few trees to climb back in Queens, but this made climbing the few trees there were a point of pride for all of the neighborhood kids. Out of all of them: Cynthia had been the best. Even though she was one of the smallest children, she compensated by being both quick and fearless. Having mixed-race parents probably helped, too: it gave little Cynthia something to prove to the all-white and all-black kids.

So now she scrambled to the top of the tree, just as she had done when she was a child. She broke through the canopy and was temporarily blinded by the blazing late-morning sun. As she looked out over the jungle, Cynthia was glad that she made the climb. If she'd run a few hundred yards further, she would have been on the beach.

The hooting resumed in the jungle below. Umberto was closer to her now, but from the sound of it he was unaccompanied. Denny was probably through reloading the camera by now, with Tito probably still holding Jacque at gunpoint. At least there had been no more gunshots, she thought. That probably meant that Jacque was still alive. *Unless Umberto chopped him up into tiny pieces.* She hated herself for the thought.

She would not break down. She would not stop hoping or fighting.

Wrapping her hand around the base of a large branch, she used one foot to break it off. A club to defend herself. The snap was muffled, but still loud enough that it was possible Umberto may have heard it below.

She tried to swing the branch, keeping one arm around the tree for support. It wasn't going to beat a machete, that was for sure, but it was better than nothing. It was smaller than a Louisville Slugger, but so jagged and pointed at the broken end that she contemplated for a moment whether it wouldn't make a better spear than a club.

The footsteps were close now. How had Umberto been able to track her path so closely? She felt herself go faint. Maybe he could smell her. Worse, maybe she had left some kind of trail for him to follow as she blundered through the foliage of the forest floor.

Umberto had changed somehow. Maybe he'd tapped into something beyond his normal neuralgic capacity. Maybe whatever had made him crazy had upped his competency level. She held her breath as she listened to his approach. She wondered whether the leaves of her hiding-tree would be enough to conceal her, or whether her body would cast a big obvious shadow onto the pathway below.

She gripped her makeshift bat as Umberto circled the area below her. He was no longer laughing or howling now, but sniffing the air like a bloodhound. He downed the atmosphere in big gulps: he knew she was nearby.

She held the point of the branch down towards him and considered jumping from her hiding spot and attempting to skewer him to the ground with her spear. Even if she were able to hit him, the impact would probably kill her, too.

Instead, she decided to wait.

Through the wall of leaves, she could only see glimpses of him. She could tell that he still wore his boar-headdress and pig-skin cape, but his loincloth must have come undone during the chase. His semi-flaccid bloodstained manhood flapped against his thigh as he marched around the base of the tree in circles. It was the least sexy thing that Cynthia had ever seen.

He rooted through the ferns and bushes that surrounded the area, figuring that she must be lying down in the roughage to conceal herself. After he had done this twice, he screamed something in Italian. She didn't know what he said, but his words were laced with frustration. He kicked up clouds of dirt and looked from above like an overgrown spoiled child.

Naked and miffed, he walked back towards the village the way he came. She watched him as he walked, searching the forest floor for his loincloth and finding it right before moving out beyond her sight.

Same old Umberto, Cynthia thought and allowed herself the briefest of smiles.

Chapter 15
Tito

When Umberto had first walked out of the forest wearing the pig cape, Tito's initial reaction was abject terror. Not because Umberto looked dangerous or deranged, but because the Golden Guinea was interrupting such a beautiful shot.

As Umberto gripped Daria by the hair, Tito was overjoyed by the actor's dedication to this film, and his newfound panache for improvisation.

The feelings of frustration and joy were not new to Tito.

It was only when the chopping started that the unfamiliar emotions took hold.

The humanist in Tito recognized how unnatural it all was, how contrary to everything he had ever witnessed on a professional movie set (and he had been on many). There was a certain indefinable primitive *reality* to it. Jacque had vomited in response, and Tito couldn't blame him for that. The adrenaline rush had almost been too much for himself to handle.

But as Denny pushed the camera in for a closer look, and Tito began to shout "cut," Tito heard a voice at his ears. The voice was not distinguishable from his own, but still alien in a way. "This movie has just gone from good to great," it said.

As wrong as the feeling was—and it was *wrong*—he agreed with the voice. This shot: this was Tito Bronze's Odessa Steps. All his life he had wanted to achieve this level of pure cinema…and now he'd done it.

This was the sequence that would outlive him, the one that he would be remembered for. It would be studied by scholars and critics until the end of time.

So when the camera had run out of film and Jacque was about to do something drastic—possibly kill his star—Tito had acted to protect the remainder of his film. He thumbed back the hammer on the Korovin and pointed the small gun in Jacque's face.

Get one thing straight: Tito wasn't condoning murder. He wasn't ready to perpetrate murder. He was only trying to secure his cinematic legacy.

"What are you doing?" Jacque asked, flashing a panicked look behind Tito. Tito ignored his question and turned the gun on his little actress squeeze.

Tito was a mediocre filmmaker, but he was an excellent marksman. He could have taken her out, but they needed her to complete the film.

Umberto may have been covered in layers of human and pig blood, but he was still an actor. Actors are cattle and should be treated as such, or whatever it was that Hitchcock had said.

"Catch her," he shouted at him. Much to his relief, Umberto listened and ran off into the jungle instead of attacking and killing Tito. The actor may have lost his mind, but he still knew who was writing the checks.

Tito put the gun back on Jacque. "Why are you doing this?" the negro asked.

How could he not see it? Was he not an educated man? Didn't he see that what they were doing was creating supreme art? They hadn't set out to do it. They had set out to make money, but now art was happening all the same.

Tito thought it best not to answer him. A man must come to these kind of realizations on his own.

After a few minutes away, Denny returned with the camera. "Latest reel safely reloaded, boss. We're ready to roll."

Boss: that was a new development. Maybe Denny had learned some respect after that last sequence. Maybe the call of true art was too strong for even a know-it-all brat like Denny.

"We can't go yet. We need the girl."

"Well she'll definitely be back on set in a minute," Denny said. "Where should I be setting up? Should I be getting pickups and inserts?"

"Get all the coverage you can," Tito said. He was no longer annoyed that the boy was trying to call the shots. It was good that Denny was showing such initiative. "I'm going to have a talk with our screenwriter about where the story goes from here."

Denny gave him a salute and turned to around to face Daria's body. He held a hand out and began to take light readings above her mangled corpse.

Tito tried to look Jacque in the eye, but the writer was trying to avoid his gaze. He spoke anyway.

"A writer who doesn't produce isn't a writer, Jacque," Tito said to him in French. It was a language that seemed tailor-made for pontification. Tito was happy that he got to use it while talking to Jacque.

The black man's eyes were plastered to the barrel of the gun in front of his face. He followed the bouncing ball as Tito waved it around.

"I know that you understand this, but there is a firm hierarchy on a film set. It's a delicate chain of symbiosis in which all the links have to be maintained if our work is to reach pure cinema."

"Can I at least be allowed to sit down while I listen to this crazy horseshit?" Jacque asked.

Tito flipped the Korovin around, careful to keep his finger off the trigger. He pointed the butt at Jacque, raised up on his toes and pistol-whipped him over his left eyebrow. The blow sent the black man to the ground. The gun may have been small, but it was heavy.

"You think I'm joking with you? Do you want to ruin what we can achieve here? If you do, just say so and I'll put a bullet through your eye. Well, I'll do it in a moment, once Denny gets the tripod set up."

"Don't," Jacque said, wavering as he propped himself up with his elbows. Tito looked beyond him now, to the space right behind the fire. He could see them all: the people of the island. They stood in a semi-circle, nodding their approval to Tito, their feet facing behind them. This film would be dedicated to their memory.

The vision collapsed as Umberto bounded through the tall grass and into camp. He was empty-handed except for the blade.

"Where is she?" Tito looked at him and the actor just shrugged. Mr. Hitchcock was right: *cattle*.

Chapter 16
Cynthia

What had happened to the men of the crew? Or at least the *white men*, Cynthia thought, her arm sore from hugging the tree. She remembered something her grandmother (the darker one) had once told her. She laughed at the thought.

"I love your granddad," her grandmother had said. "But every single white man I have ever met is either one of two things: hateful or crazy." Her grandfather had fallen firmly into the 'crazy' category, but Cynthia had also noted that after too many drinks he was known to dabble in hatefulness, even though her grandma would never admit to it.

Not content with folksy life lessons, Cynthia's grandmother was also fond of telling her stories from her life back in Trinidad. Cynthia remembered parts of those stories now with a frown, wishing she was on *that* Caribbean island instead.

Maybe the answer to today's violence lay in her grandmother's stories. Tales of Obeah, the folkloric religion that the grandmothers in Trinidad used to practice in secret, and that the Christian preachers used to warn the kids about.

From what her grandmother had told her, it was a religion full of evil ghosts and lost spirits. It sounded great for getting the little kids in Trinidad to behave, but beyond that it had sounded hokey.

She thought about the mass grave.

What better source of lost souls could there be?

It didn't much matter. The cause could have been vengeful spirits on loan from Trinidad, residual radiation from atomic tests that had driven the white men insane, or even something as mundane as dysentery from the well water. Whatever the reason, the makeup girl was still sans her head.

Forgetting herself, Cynthia yawned and stretched out her arm. Instantly, she was catapulted forward in her seat. She regained her grip, but not before the momentary feeling of falling that accompanied being confronted with such a height.

Cynthia's vision swam as she scrutinized the jungle floor from her perch in the tree. There was no movement. She listened. No sounds except for the occasional bird.

Getting up the tree had been an easier proposition than getting down would be. Going up there had been no choice. She either climbed or she was murdered by an Italian B-lister.

After Umberto had left, she waited fifteen minutes to make sure that he wasn't still searching the area. Then she thought of a plan for another fifteen minutes. At least she estimated they were fifteen minutes increments: at the rate her mind was working they could have been anywhere between three minutes to an hour.

The sun was directly overhead when she made the decision to climb down. The orbital fireball was her only reliable way of marking time. She felt guilty for leaving Jacque for so long. She further saddened herself with the thought that Jacque's chances for survival already seemed bleak, and whatever aide Cynthia could give him had much less chance for success with each passing second. Or did it? What could she possibly do for him in the daytime? She was out-gunned, out-numbered and out-crazied.

First things first: whatever plans she would be employing would be contingent on getting out of the tree alive. She reached the lowest branch, threw her weapon down to the dirt below and watched as it splintered in half from the fall.

That could be my legs, she thought. Holding her breath and swinging her arms out to grasp the trunk.

The second step was a doozy. She miscalculated, and the ground below sped up to greet her.

Cut to black.

Chapter 17

Denny

For most of the day, Denny had filmed Umberto alone with the girl's corpse. In close-up and medium shot, Tito and Denny had watched Umberto strip the remainder of the girl's clothes, slit open her insides, and run his hand along her bones.

"Now eat her guts." Tito had urged him on while Denny pushed in. After Tito had deemed that they had gone as far as they could with one cannibal, he insisted that Denny get into costume.

It was a common industry joke that everything on a set is held together by gaffer's tape, but that didn't make it any less true. Denny not only used it to secure Jacque's hands and feet, but also when Umberto started carving up the makeup girl and passing around trophies. Denny used the strong black tape to form a necklace for himself, stringing Daria's ears and nose around his naked chest.

Every shot couldn't be handheld. That would have been tacky. Besides, there were so few of them now that Denny would have to be part of the cast: the tripod had become a necessity.

He'd worked on a bunch of films, but this was the first time he'd been in one.

Tito had cast him in the part of a cannibal. To darken his skin, Denny had mixed up some of the makeup girl's blood with the dark soil of the jungle. The mud wasn't going to make him look as black as Jacque, but it did look considerable better than his white undershirt and cargo shorts.

The camera ran behind Denny and Umberto, capturing their invented ritual. Denny had framed a wide shot and then closed down the viewfinder so he could let the camera roll by itself without exposing the film.

Umberto picked up one of Daria's hands. Her joints had begun to stiffen in the hours since this morning's death scene.

The blonde Italian raised his blade and cut off three of her fingers with one fluid swipe. Umberto bent to collect them, popping one into his mouth like a cigarette and offering another to Denny.

Dennis Roth, professional cinematographer, would never resort to cannibalism. But he was too deep in character now, and they were already using up film for this shot.

There were plenty of similar moments like this in other films. But those movies didn't have the balls to go all the way. The furthest *Cannibal Fury Atrocity* had gone was the on-screen slaughter of a few animals.

That's child's play, Denny thought. *We can beat that!*

Denny took the meat from Umberto and sucked on the jagged circular wound at the end of the finger.

In his off-screen life, Dennis had once taken a trip to New Orleans with his parents and while there he had dined on a crawfish boil. The most important part, the waitress had told him, was after you were done with the meat inside the chest of the crawfish, that you had to suck on the head to get all of the juices out.

Sucking on Daria's finger reminded him of this. He'd heard method actors tried to recall particularly vivid sense memories to help themselves get into character. Denny tried it now and hoped that the emotion would translate to the screen.

Sucking, Denny couldn't help but note that the girl's

marrow lacked the Cajun spice of the crawfish, but it was not devoid of flavor. He tried nibbling a bit of the outer flesh. The salt from Daria's dried sweat mingled nicely on his palate with the alkaloid tang of her blood. Not bad.

Just out of frame, Jacque moaned and snapped awake. Denny watched out of his peripheral vision as the black man struggled against the gaff tape that bound his arms to his side. His body was then thatched to a tall wooden stake. The pole must have been used by the natives to hang up their fishing nets, because it was studded with several small hooks.

Jacque's eyes were wandering and unfocused for a moment before going wide as he caught sight of what Umberto and Denny were doing to Daria's body. His screams would have ruined the shot if they had been rolling sound.

"Quiet on set," Tito said, appearing from the hut beside Jacque. He'd been standing just inside the doorway, watching them, occasionally whispering to himself.

At least Denny assumed he was talking to himself. There was no way of knowing whether or not he was speaking directly to the people of the island. Denny knew they only revealed themselves when they wanted to, but he guessed that they were around them constantly. They were omnipresent spectral producers and investors, watching their film come to blazing Technicolor life.

"Cut," Tito shouted. Denny walked over to the camera and switched it off, still gnawing the finger. Lee Strasberg's method was growing on him.

"Looks like it will be getting dark in a few, anyway," Denny said, disappointment heavy in his voice. With no electricity, there would be no way to use the lights they had carried with them off the plane and into the town.

Tomorrow, they would have to shoot day-for-night if they wanted nighttime scenes in their movie. There was no way they were going to be able to get the fire bright enough that it could effectively light a shot. There was no point in Denny telling this to Tito. The man was a pro and he already knew.

"Strike the equipment for the day, then, and reload the camera," Tito said to Denny. "And you," he indicated Umberto and began speaking in Italian.

Umberto squinted with his good eye and wiped his bloody hands on his chest, smearing the intricate tribal designs that he had spent most of the day adding to. He had used both stage paint and Daria's blood to make the designs, and they read well behind the lens. But it was going to be very difficult to keep proper continuity with their makeup if they kept changing it. Especially now that they'd killed the makeup girl.

Umberto lumbered off into the jungle. He still walked with power, but the spring was gone from his step after a long day of work.

"I'm assuming you told him to go out and search for our starlet," Denny said, casually rubbing at his bare arms. He was no longer self-conscious about his track marks, and they peeked out from underneath the dried mud as it flaked away with his scratching.

On the island, Denny didn't have to hide who he was. He could not only be himself, but be who he'd always wanted to be. The thought comforted his mind, but did little to stop the itch in his veins.

"After you're done here, you'll be going out with him." Tito motioned to the setup, indicating what Denny already knew: that he had to stow the camera, film and equipment for the night.

Chapter 18
Cynthia

She awoke in the dark, with the taste of dead leaves and dried blood in her mouth. Her neck hurt as she rolled onto her side and tried to swallow.

Something sharp pushed its way down her esophagus, causing her to gag in pain and nausea. She'd chipped one of her bottom teeth, and now realized that she must have just gulped down the sharp enamel shard.

Her head throbbed and fizzed as she got to her feet. She did so carefully, not wanting to find out that she had shattered an ankle by putting all her weight on it. The darkness around her was absolute, and it was impossible to tell how long she'd been unconscious.

She was alive and alone: for that she was thankful.

Around her, the ever-present sounds of the jungle had continued on into the night. Insects continued their perpetual hum, which was now complemented by the occasional night bird coo.

Cynthia rolled her tongue along the inside of her mouth, collecting up a wad of gritty debris and spitting it out onto the ground. She tried to blow her nose into her hand, but the pain staggered her. Leaning on the nearest tree trunk for support, she brought a hand up to her face.

Before she could pull the snakes of dried blood from her

broken nose, there were footsteps in the distance.

Luckily, stealth was not Umberto's forte. Not only did he crack branches and drag his feet, but every few moments he would jibber something angry to himself in Italian. The only one of his words she understood was "moolie", and it sent an instant flash of rage to tingle her cheeks.

Even with her face smashed in and a stomach full of earth, Cynthia was able to sneak around Umberto easily. Keeping a large distance and moving quietly, she doubled back over the path he blazed towards the beach until she could see the campfire.

Falling to her belly, she crept up to the village from behind the densest row of huts. From where she stopped in the brush, it was too difficult to tell if anyone was moving around in the camp. The modest fire threw out shadows that danced and jumped in rhythms and patterns that just *might* have been human.

With economy, she began moving again. She could see the stake and Jacque lashed to it. She sped up her army-woman crawl for a moment, but slowed herself as she remembered that Tito and Denny could still be anywhere.

Then she saw the lump of meat and clothing, taking it all in before she realized what it was, before she could look away.

The meat pile was Daria.

Keep moving. Don't look at her. Don't think about her.

In a few more moments, she was under the back window of one of the huts. Something crawled across her face. There was something right below her eye and she slapped a hand up to brush the insect away.

It wasn't a bug. It was a teardrop.

She rubbed her eyes, making the pain in her face ten times worse and soaking her hands in dirty tears. She had tried not to look at what they'd done, tried to block it out, but the damage was done.

She spread them thin with her fingers, and her tears began to dry in the warm night air. Evaporation took its course as they cooled to nothingness, burning into the skin of her hands and face as Cynthia swore to herself that what happened to Daria would not happen to her.

Not making a sound, she crawled into the window to the hut and began to look for a weapon.

Chapter 19
Denny

Getting enough sleep was possibly the most important habit to get into on a film set. It was so easy to over-extend yourself during the first few days and wind up paying for it at the end of the shoot. A tired D.P. was one that made mistakes: focus slipped, footage counters went unread, and light readings weren't taken as frequently as they should be.

So instead of traipsing around the jungle looking for the girl, Denny had decided to disobey Tito's instructions and catch up on his sleep. He'd left the camp through the patch of tall grass to the west, but circled back around and crawled into one of the unused huts to get some rest.

The excitement of the day combined with the hut's uncomfortable hay and grass bedding resulted in a profound restlessness for the first few moments. Denny stared up at the low thatched ceiling of the hut and tried in vain to resist the urge to plan out a shot list for the morning.

Denny was drunk on the work…no, maybe not drunk: high on the thrill of creation. The power of the footage was intoxicating. It was a drug that heightened his senses and quickened his pulse. He'd been training his whole life for a project like this, something that had the capacity to be significant.

He shifted his weight on the bunk, and the light groan of the wood made him keenly aware of his surroundings. Fatigue overrode his excitement, and he began to relax and drift off to sleep.

I'm not on a set. This is all real. People are really being hurt. The realization loomed large and terrible in his sleepy mind for a moment before it was pushed away by images of sold-out crowds at the Film Forum in New York, and the golden glow of festival prizes.

Sometimes people get hurt for their art, he tried to rationalize.

Before he could debate the topic further with his semi-conscious self, he was knocked fully awake by the sound of something crawling into the hut via the window.

His body went rigid against the bed and he held his breath, frightened in the dark, and suddenly with an acute awareness that they were all alone in the middle of the jungle. The volume of every sound in the small hut was cranked to maximum. Outside, the fire's hisses and pops were amplified by the emptiness of the village.

Were there tigers on the small island, other predatory animals that he'd never even heard of? The horror was immediate and primitive: he was a simple Stone Age man, shrinking from shadows.

Denny tried to remain calm and soundless as he turned his head to see what had sloughed in through the small window. His eyes had adjusted to the dank hut, but they didn't have to, because Cynthia's bleach-blonde hair was almost phosphorescent in the darkness.

She was right there! Denny wanted to laugh and shout, or at least heave with relief, but he stopped himself. Umberto was probably making laps around the camp with his dick in his hand, and here she was stumbling through Denny's hut.

She either hadn't seen the bed, or hadn't seen him because his brown tribal makeup was camouflaging him. With her back turned to him, she leafed through the baskets and tangles of fishing nets piled against the opposite wall of the hut.

She would notice him soon: he would have to make his move if he was going to do it. As soon as he stirred, she would hear the groan of the bunk, so what was his plan? Knock her down and out, and then tie her up with her boyfriend.

Without moving his head, Denny swept the room with his eyes, looking for something he could use as a club. There was nothing, unless he wanted to pry a leg off the bed, but by that point he would lose the element of surprise.

His hands instinctively floated up to the light meter slung around his chest, and gripped onto the totem for comfort. He didn't usually sleep with it, but tonight he was glad he did.

Careful to make as little sound as possible, he looped the fabric from around his neck and hefted the light meter in one hand. It was a solid lump of polished metal. It would be much more useful than nothing.

Here. We. Go.

He leapt up from the bed, his lower back mewling at the sudden movement, and both feet sending up a cloud of dirt as they hit the dry ground of the hut. As soon as he was confident he wasn't going to topple over, he took a big step.

He lunged forward, the light meter held high and ready to slam down on the back of the girl's head. Denny hesitated for a split-second, unsure how much force to use to knock her out, not wanting to kill her. Was he strong enough to kill her? He hoped not.

Before he could lower his hand, the girl whirled around. There was shock and a stunning level of ferocity gouged into her dark, pretty face.

Then there was a tug in Denny's chest, and *everything*, even the fire and jungle outside, went silent.

The only sound that filled his ears was his own breathing.

He loosened his grip, and the light meter—his most

prized possession, even more than his fix kit—hit the ground.

"My, my," he started to speak, his words frantic but hushed. His eyes darted down to his chest.

The actress's hand was still wrapped around the hilt of the small knife.

The villager who lived here had probably used the knife to unravel his nets and debone fish, but now the blade was between Denny's ribs, right over his heart.

"Don't." He tried to say something about removing the knife. He'd read in a book once that it was only when you removed an impalement that you were in real trouble.

Cynthia shushed him. "I'm sorry," she said. "I know this wasn't your fault." There were tears in her eyes.

She kept one hand on the knife and cradled Denny with the other. She helped him lay back on the ground with minimal effort, her muscles straining against his skinny frame.

"Who…" Denny tried to speak to the figures that had gathered above him, the ones whose backwards feet were not touching the ground. Cynthia put her free hand over his mouth and pressed her fingers against his lips, silencing him.

There was a flash of crimson as she pulled out the knife, and his still-beating heart sent a warm pool of blood out over the front of his shirt.

She kept both her hands over his mouth and stayed with him until he drifted off to sleep.

Denny began to dream of those long nights and thrills on 42nd Street. The movies, both great and terrible, and their starlets, both beautiful and tragic, flooded over his fading consciousness.

Before he faded completely, Denny realized that one day Cynthia was going to be a star.

Chapter 20

Jacque

It might have been some combination of blood loss, exhaustion, and the warm hypnotic glow of the fire. Whatever the reason, Jacque passed into a deep sleep right after Tito had stopped raving at him.

The director had wanted an updated script, one that incorporated the recent changes in the production (i.e. the majority of the crew turning into raving murderous lunatics). Although he'd threatened to, Jacque guessed that Tito probably wouldn't shoot him without the camera rolling. Refusing to give him story ideas had not stopped Tito's creative juices from flowing, though.

"In that fucking Italian piece of shit—the one that we are ripping off—they got in big trouble for impaling a girl. Big trouble means big box office, free press, underground status." Tito waxed rhapsodically in French, his words moving his wheels until he'd revved himself into a frenzy of creation. "So how do we top that?" he asked Jacque, and continued before he could answer: "We impale a girl upside down! Instead of having the stake hidden underneath her ass, where you can't see it, we have it come out somewhere else!"

Jacque saw where this line of reasoning was going to end up. He also knew who Tito intended to be the impalee: Cynthia.

"Nobody will be able to figure out how we did it, how we achieved the effect."

"Because you're so crazy you'll actually do it," Jacque said, leaning forward against his restraints. No use. If he was going to help Cynthia, it wasn't going to be by breaking out of the loops of gaffer's tape binding his chest and hands.

"That's the beauty of it: nobody knows that we're actually going to do it. Cinéma vérité! The world's first Neo-realist splatter movie."

"De Sica just used non-actors and real bombed-out locations. He didn't kill off his cast. They'll know it when half the crew goes missing, when our families come looking for us."

"What family?" Tito asked, knowing the answer. Someone would miss the girl's, at least, but Jacque was tired of arguing with a madman.

"Sure. Sounds great. You're a chin-e-matic genius," Jacque said; and after a few more moments of rambling, Tito left him alone to fall asleep.

His sleep was deep enough for dreams.

•

In his dreams, he met the people of the island. They didn't talk to him. He learned everything he would know about them by feeling and intuition, the way you're sure of something in a dream without it being made explicit.

There were many of them. Most of them were black, but there were some whites with shaggy looking beards and crazy eyes, as well.

Jacque knew that they were stuck there: dead, angry and bored. They weren't especially malevolent. It was hard to look tough when your leader is a little old lady, but what was going on now was their duty. They'd made an oath a very long time ago, and they were going to stick to it.

The old woman looked like Jacque's grandmother, only she wore ropes of shells and bones around her neck, and her feet were twisted to face behind her.

She raised her hand and frowned, ready to say something, maybe even apologize.

But before she could speak, Jacque was jolted back into reality.

•

Cold wet tendrils wrapped themselves around his wrist, and he let out a gasp. The bloody hand that was fumbling with the gaffer's tape stopped what it was doing and shot up to his mouth.

"Quiet," Cynthia whispered in his ear. "I'm getting you loose. But I don't know where Tito is."

The sudden tenseness of his spine went slack when he realized it was her, that she was alive and setting him free.

"Don't move or I'll slip and cut you, I'm shaking enough already." She spoke so low and cautiously that she had to touch his ear with her lips just to be heard.

There was a snip as she poked at the restraints with her blade, and then a tearing sound as she ripped the tape the rest of the way.

His arms were free. But instead of relief came a numbness in his burnt hands and a dull pain at his shoulders. However long he'd been tied to the stake, it had been long enough for his bound arms to atrophy into jelly.

Jacque turned to face her, the sudden burst of blood coursing back into his extremities, causing a moment of double-vision and light-headedness. She was covered in blood and dirt.

"What happened?" he asked. The pained look on her face tried to remind him to keep his voice down.

"I fell out of a tree," she said, offering a faint enough smile that he could see the jagged gap where a tooth had once been. She looked at the blood on her hands. "And I killed Dennis. Did I have to do that?" Her question caught him off guard.

"It's us or them," Jacque offered in reply, but it sounded stupid as he said it. Who knew if Denny hadn't just been in a state of shock when he'd been filming Daria's murder? Maybe he was just playing along with Tito and Umberto because not doing so would have gotten him tied to the stake behind Jacque.

There was no going back from dead. He tried not to think about it.

"You had to," he said, hoping it was the truth. Cynthia looked like she needed him to be sure, so he tried to sound it. "Tito is definitely off the deep end."

"Then let's get out of here." Cynthia hooked and arm under his shoulder and began to pull. "Can you stand?"

She wasn't giving him much of a choice, so he tried it. His joints stung as if someone had wrapped them in barbed wire while he was asleep, but he got to his feet and was able to lean against the stake.

The fire was dying down now, and it gave everything a soft orange glow, but little illumination.

"Where are we going?" Jacque needed to know, because her plan was oblique at best.

"If we head into the jungle, we'll be able to hear them coming." She was choosing her words and pulling him along as she whispered.

"Not that way. Over here, we need water. The well." Jacque pulled back against her and wished he hadn't. The strain between his arm and shoulder almost made him scream out in anguish.

Cynthia mouthed a silent "sorry" and followed him to the far side of the village, ducking low to the ground and trying to move in the shadows cast by the huts. The crouching was not only a burden on Jacque's cramped-up legs and back, but altogether useless for avoiding Tito.

"Stop right there!" Tito's voice boomed out in English. There was not even a hint of his cartoon accent in the words. "I'm through wasting bullets on warning shots. The next time I pull this trigger, I'm putting one in your skull, Jacky boy." The last part was in French except for "Jacky Boy."

Jacque didn't turn to face Tito. The old man was already out of breath from shouting, and it sounded like there was a solid distance between them. Squeezing Cynthia's hand hurt, but he had to do it to get her attention.

"Don't listen to him. We make a run for it. And when I drop your hand, you split to the right and head for the trees."

He gave her one look, long enough to see her eyes gently pleading.

And then they ran forward together.

Chapter 21
Tito

Tito Bronze was a veteran director with over thirty films in his oeuvre. Over forty, if you counted the porno movies and stag loops that he'd done under the name "Terrance Amato." Tito Bronze was a professional.

Tito Bronze did not bluff.

He did not bluff, but he had not expected the crazy writer to start running away, either. It took a moment to widen his stance and level the gun. Between the inconsistent light, Jacque's bobbing gait, and his reluctance to hit the girl, the first shot went wild.

There was a small explosion of dirt and debris in front of the black man, and he loosened his grip on the girl's hand in response. Already the pair was disappearing deeper into the village, zigzagging at odd intervals and trying their best to mess up Tito's aim.

He decided that he could use their indirect path to his advantage if he ran straight forward. The fastest route was always a straight line. Tito began to hobble after them, his lungs burning with exertion and heavy with the tar of too many cigarettes.

Cynthia began to peel away into the jungle and Tito let her go. They could always catch the girl again. He had no real way of stopping her, and no hope of catching her on foot. Besides, Tito had promised that he would shoot Jacque, so he kept after the black man.

Tito felt his gut jiggle with each step, wishing he were just a bit closer so he could put one in the base of Jacque's neck. Intentionally winging Jacque to keep him alive was an option, but there was too little time for trick shots. His target was approaching the tall grass, his dark skin getting harder to spot as they moved further away from the fire and into the inky blackness of night.

Jacque made a jerky motion, as if he were jumping over a small hurtle. *He thinks jumping is going to save him.* The thought amused Tito as he leveled the weapon. Now was as close as he was ever going to be.

He exhaled and took two more long strides. On the third step, he squeezed the trigger.

As the ground gave way underneath him.

The well. The fucking well.

It was a primitive hole in the ground with no real covering, and no warning that it was there. There didn't have to be. All the villagers had probably warned their children often not to play near it.

Tito heard his own yelp as his gut slammed into the far side of the hole, crumbling the dirt around the edge and knocking the breath out of him. As his feet kept falling, he threw out his arms in a desperate attempt to grab a hold of the edge.

He balled his hands into a fist, and the gun went off again, jumping out of his hand and onto the dirt at the mouth of the hole. Both elbows crashed against the edge, his hands flailing, fingers ripping at the ground, trying to pull him back on to solid ground.

Struggling caused more harm than good. Tito snapped off the fingernail on his left index finger.

Then plummeted into claustrophobic darkness.

Chapter 22
Umberto

From the beach, through his good eye, Umberto could see the faintest corona of light as it stretched across the watery horizon.

The coming dawn made him wonder how long he had been out in the jungle, looking for the girl.

At one point in the night he had heard something, but the movement seemed to come from all directions at once. So by the time he mustered the energy he needed for pursuit, popping a pill down his dry throat and rushing off into the foliage, the night was again at rest.

When he heard the gunshot, he was preparing to give up the search, collapse into the sand and let the sunrise warm him. His bare feet were numb from running. Last night, he'd taken off his boots and used the laces to affix the boar head to the top of his own. The rest of his body was numb from the fistfuls of uppers and downers marinating with the bits of makeup girl-flesh in his stomach.

Running made the mixture in his stomach slosh around like a caged animal, but it didn't exactly make him sick.

Umberto couldn't believe he ate so much. At first he was just rolling the meat around in his mouth, but then he decided that when the footage was played back in a theater—three stories tall, just mouthing the blood and guts wasn't going to read as authentic. So he'd swallowed some, then a bit more.

The people pressing against his mind urged him on with every bite and lick.

Tito was the only one with a gun. Tito was never going to leave the comfort of the village. Thus Umberto concluded that the gunshot had to have come from the village. At a full sprint, the assemblage of huts and fishing nets was still a minimum of ten minutes from the beach.

A second shot, closer but still far, rang out through the woods and quickened his footfalls. Umberto bounded over fallen trees and through a number of deep mud puddles that could have just as easily been quicksand.

He wasn't running because he wanted to protect the cameraman and director—he could give a shit—but to protect the project. Umberto had already given up so much over the last two days (not only out of his schedule, but possibly out of his soul): he intended on collecting the fame that he had been promised.

How long since you've slept? a familiar voice asked at the back of his mind, he almost didn't recognize it at first. It had been so long since he had heard his own voice in his head.

It had been a long time since he'd been asleep. The last time had been on the plane. It did not feel like it had been that much time, but it was.

As suddenly as it had arrived, the voice of reason departed. The now-familiar chorus of the island raised its voice until there was no more of Umberto left.

They told him to keep running.

As he hit the packed dirt roads of the village, it took tremendous effort to will his arms and legs to stop moving. His skid into town left a trail of dust in his wake like the perpetual cloud that followed Speedy Gonzales.

There had been two gunshots, but there were no bodies

and blood that Umberto could see. He looked around in the first morning light. There was no one at all: living or dead.

"Pronto," Umberto asked into the emptiness of the village. What had happened here, and where was the moolie? The wooden stake was empty, the remnants of Jacque's tape restraints still stuck to the sides.

There was a groan and Umberto whirled around, muscles painfully tensing as he readied himself for attack.

There was nothing behind him, no one that he could see.

"Aiuto!" The voice was calling from right in front of him, but Umberto still saw nothing.

"Signore Bronze," Umberto asked the empty clearing. The director's voice was recognizable, but weak. There were no more cries for help, only quick labored breaths.

Then Umberto's eyes fell on the hole in the ground, the small pistol lying right in front of it, and all at once he pieced together what must have happened.

A jail break? Really?

How could the "legendary" Tito Bronze be so stupid?

The sunrise was almost complete now, but the morning haze resulted in heavy shadows. Umberto had to cup his eye as he peered over the edge of the well.

"What happened to you?" Umberto asked. He was only able to make out the tip of Tito's silver beard staring up at him from the blackness of the well.

Below, the old man gave a wet cough and moaned as he cleared some phlegm, and possibly blood. His body didn't seem far enough down to be at the bottom of the well. The fat old bastard was probably stuck halfway, wedged between the coarse sheets of limestone as they angled closer together.

"Throw me the bucket. Pull me up," Tito wheezed. It was apparent that he was expending great energy just to say a few words.

"How badly are you hurt?" Umberto asked, ignoring the director's demands for the time being.

"I'm fine. Throw me the rope and pull me up!" The scream came at great cost. Umberto could hear the crumbling of rock as Tito's body wedged itself deeper into the hole.

"No," Umberto said. "It won't hold you."

"Yes, it will."

"I'm not strong enough to pull you up," Umberto said.

His mind was now made up. The old woman with the shell necklace spoke to him, reminded him of how badly Tito Bronze had harmed his career. Tito had put him in schlock, picture after picture. For Tito Bronze, Umberto was a joke.

This man was no friend of his.

"Mr. big action star, not strong enough? No!" Tito tried to sound chummy, but there was too much desperation in his voice to sound anything but terrified and anguished.

Umberto's response was moving away from the edge.

"That's my boy," Tito said, from down in the hole.

Umberto picked up the Korovin and put it in the waistband of his loincloth. With his foot, he edged the water basket further away from the mouth of the pit.

"I'm going to wake Denny and have him get the camera," Umberto said.

"What for? Where's the rope?" Tito was beginning to sound desperate. Umberto ignored him and went looking for the camera.

He was going to finish this movie by himself.

Chapter 23
Cynthia

She'd been close enough to know that Tito's first shot was a miss. As the bullet whizzed by, Jacque let go of her hand.

That was her signal to run off into the jungle. And she did, not able to look back for the second shot, and the pained scream that immediately followed it.

The foliage bordering the village was thicker in this area, her feet were being torn up with every step, but still she ran. If Jacque had been shot to buy her an extra few moments to escape, Cynthia was not going to let his sacrifice be in vain.

After running until the trees were tall and the canopy dark above her, she turned and listened. There had been no more gunshots, but there wasn't any sound from Jacque's foot-falls, either.

Her face throbbed, her feet bled, but still she was able to summon her newfound jungle-walking abilities to make a sound-less trek back to the west side of the village: the place where Jacque should have broken through the tall grass and into the jungle to meet with her.

The treeline thinned as she approached the village, and she watched the sunrise begin in the east. She held her breath as she walked and let it out in small, quiet bursts as she surveyed the empty village.

She got close enough to see that the small panels that

had been laid on top of the well were missing. That had been Jacque's plan, and it looked like it had worked, Tito's small pistol teetering on the edge of the hole.

She allowed herself a smile, an expression that felt both grotesque and triumphant as it stretched across her face.

"Hey." His shaky voice made her jump in surprise. She had Jacque wrapped up in her arms before he could say anymore.

"We did it," was all she said before the wetness of the embrace stopped her.

She looked down at her filthy blouse, now soaked in blood.

Jacque's blood.

"No." Her own voice sounded small and defeated. It made tears blur her vision.

"I'm alright," Jacque said. She daubed her eyes, turned him around, and saw that he was either lying or wrong. There was a small dark hole below his left shoulder blade, the flesh around it puckered and bruised.

The gunshot was close to his spine, heart and lungs. It oozed as she placed her hand next to it, only applying the slightest pressure. Jacque gave a quick hiss in response.

There was no exit wound in his chest. The bullet was still rattling around in there, and she wasn't going to go digging for it with the tiny blade she'd used to kill Denny.

Still holding him tight, feeling the warmth of his body as it began to fade under her palms, she pushed him to the forest floor. She helped him flatten the sharp grass beneath his back and lower himself to the ground. They were very close to the outskirts of town; but with Denny dead and Tito at least incapacitated, there was only one very loud person they had to keep an ear out for.

"Tito fell in the well," Jacque said, giving a faint laugh

and smiling. His mouth was speckled with blood, like a girl who'd mistakenly smudged lipstick all over her front teeth.

"I know, good job," Cynthia said as she packed fallen leaves under his wound, letting Jacque's body weight do the work of applying the pressure. This probably wasn't the most sanitary way of dressing the wound, but it was all she had.

"I think he might have clipped me," Jacque said. His tone hadn't been this light the entire trip, and the combination of morbidity, smiles and hopelessness did something to Cynthia. She laughed, not for his benefit, but because she found genuine humor in the situation, the laughter made her tears flow faster and fiercer. They splattered Jacque's bare chest and neck.

"What's that?" Jacque said and gave her hand a firm squeeze with his blistered fingers. She had not heard Umberto enter the camp and choked as she tried to hold in her laughter and sobs.

The Italian looked even worse than the last time she'd seen him. His sunburn had begun to peel, the pink splotchy skin underneath looking alternatively leathery and inflamed. Prominent veins stuck out from his neck and arms, moving across his skin like inchworms as he walked over to the well and spoke into it.

Most of his makeup had washed away. Only his fur loincloth remained, and it had shriveled against his buttocks as the pig's flesh began to dry.

Tito spoke from the hole in Italian, but she could barely hear him, so it didn't matter that she couldn't understand him. If Umberto was able to pull his boss to safety, then the teams would be even: one wounded man to each side.

Cynthia followed Umberto's gaze to the gun. She cursed herself for not running out and picking it up while she had the chance.

Umberto stuffed the pistol in his skin-belt next to his machete, which had been cut up his thigh, leaving deep gouges as he ran. Rising to stand, Umberto kicked the basket and rope further away from the well. It didn't look to Cynthia like he was going to try helping Tito to the surface any time soon.

Jacque coughed, and she put a bloody finger to his lips, silently pleading with him to hold it in. His respiration was shallow, and his lungs sounded like they were beginning to flood.

He's going to die on this island, she thought, remembering that the plane and any hope of rescue did not arrive until tomorrow morning.

She removed her finger when it was clear that Umberto was walking away from them, back into town. Jacque's brow was beaded with a cold sweat and she brushed his hair as she watched Umberto walk through the huts, ducking inside each one, looking for something.

Finally, he reached the hut where Denny's body was stashed. Cynthia hadn't done much to hide what she'd done. She just covered Denny with the bed roll after she could not get his eyes to close.

It was hard to tell from this distance, but Umberto didn't seem surprised to find the cameraman's dead body. Instead, he stayed in the hut for a moment, and came back out with the camera propped on one shoulder.

He came back to the edge of the well and spoke in Italian some more, motioning to the camera, playing with the knobs and switches until finally it whirred to life.

Umberto pointed it up at the rising sun, then down into the hole. He spoke some more, louder this time, his voice carrying the familiar cadence of a director.

"Action!" he yelled, taking the gun from his loincloth.

He waved the end around the hole in small circles until firing once, stopping to say something, and then again. He knelt, trying to stay out of his own shadow while angling the lens down into the hole.

Cynthia didn't want to, but she gasped.

Umberto turned to her, took his eye from the viewfinder, and smiled.

Chapter 24

Umberto

Umberto hated talking to other actors. Not only were they self-absorbed, and always looking for Umberto to introduce them to Roland Pressberg or Tito Bronze, but they always said the same annoying phrases.

The one Umberto had grown to hate most was:

"What I really want to do is direct!"

Not only was it a cliché, but the men who usually said it were bad, ineffectual actors who would probably make worse directors.

Now here he was, getting his first taste of being director, writer, star and D.P. of his own film, and he wanted more. The other side of the camera was pure power.

Even more so was the gun.

Tito had begun to beg near the end, once Umberto had said "Action!" and realized what he was going to do. Umberto had dwarfed the old man, used that very special word to subsume him.

In a way, Bronze was dead before the bullets entered his face, broke out his front teeth, and exploded out the back of his head.

The sun was up now, but it was casting hard shadows, and it was still difficult to see what was going on in the hole. Umberto had cranked the exposure way up, hoping that even if the film was overexposed, Tito's frightened expression would be captured in some way.

After he shot him, Umberto made sure to get some coverage of the body, kneeling low to the ground and sticking the lens as close to Tito's face as he could get.

He had only gotten one take, but he guessed that the footage was miraculous. Finding the girl had been an added bonus, her gasp getting his attention, even with the camera still humming in his ear. Her near-platinum blond hair made her easy to spot against the greens and browns of the jungle.

All the fatigue and queasiness that had accumulated over the last few days was gone. Umberto held his head and his camera high as he ran towards the girl. He could see that she was panicked.

She was a tiny blonde fawn in his headlights, unsure whether to run or to give up.

He broke through the grass and saw why she was hesitant to run. There lying next to her was the writer, the leaves and saw-grass around him pooling with blood.

As he approached, the girl huddled over him with her arm outstretched, clutching a small blade. The corners of her eyes were impossibly white, possessing all the fury of a mother animal protecting her nest.

Umberto just shook his head. "Stupid girl, I don't want him. What kind of grand finale would it be without my co-star?"

His words were unintelligible to her, he knew that, but it didn't matter. He tightened his grip on the camera and took a step towards her, swatting away the hand that held the knife.

She grunted and screamed as his fingers reached for her scalp. The blade dug into his forearm, drawing a deep red line across his skin. There was no pain, so he continued his momentum, catching a wad of her hair and yanking her onto her backside. The knife slipped from her hand from either the blood or the shock.

The writer tried to sit up, but Umberto pushed him back down with the heel of his foot, focusing the camera on his pained expression as more pressure was applied to the wound on his back.

The girl screamed some more, no doubt pleading with Umberto to leave the dying man alone. He would indulge her, but she should have instead been begging for her own life.

He moved the end of the camera, watching with his uninjured eye through the viewfinder as the grass he was dragging her through tugged at the exposed flesh of her arms. The saw-grass left cuts on her arms that looked minuscule on film but were probably agony to endure.

Once he'd wasted enough film on her red-faced screams on the trip back to camp, he switched to a long shot of the village, the wooden stake and fire in the middle.

It was an establishing shot of where his film's final scene—the grand finale—would take place.

Chapter 25

Cynthia

She had lived through all of this for *what*?

Her scalp throbbed from where Umberto had dug his well-manicured nails in, dragging her to the center of town before lifting her off her feet and binding her by her wrists to the wooden stake by the fire. Gravity had left her arms mercifully free of sensation, her shoulders howling in pain for the first few minutes before the feeling of nothingness had spread to her whole body.

She watched as Umberto tried to figure out the tripod.

Cynthia wondered how it was possible that someone who had worked on movies for the bulk of his life was having a difficult time getting the legs even, not realizing that there was a level built into the base of the instrument to help him. She was going to be tortured and mutilated by an idiot, in all likelihood not even in focus. It figured.

After five more minutes of teaching her exotic curse words, Umberto re-shouldered the camera, deciding to go handheld for her death sequence.

As he approached her, there was a click, and the camera cranked to life.

"Action," he whispered. It was the only English she'd ever heard him speak.

He reached out a hand to her, grabbing for her shirt,

ready to rip it off of her like he did to Daria.

Daria. The thought conjured up one last morsel of reserve rage inside her.

She arched her back against the smooth, aged wood of the stake, and waited until Umberto was in range.

The sleazy Italian licked his upper lip, cleaning his amber mustache with his tongue and beginning to laugh under his breath. "Good movie," he said to her, trying to soothe but only disgusting her. "Big star." Motioning first to himself, and then to her.

The back of his hand brushed against her breast, and she let him have it, pulling herself up by the wrists and kicking him in the stomach with both feet. He doubled to the dirt. His free hand clutched the lens, more concerned with catching the camera than grabbing his stomach.

He remained crouched. His breath was labored for a moment as Cynthia wriggled against the wood, trying to rip the tape off her hands but finding it impossible to get a tear started.

Umberto hefted himself to his feet again, this time the machete filling his free hand. He didn't speak, only shook his head and gave her a slight *tsk* before laying the blade flat against her neck. She tried to shrink away from its cold touch.

But there was nowhere to go.

Umberto left the edge of the machete where it was and brought the camera so close to her face that she could see herself in its lens. Her image was bubbled and distorted, a fish-eye version of herself that she did not wholly recognize.

It wasn't just the swollen nose or the bruises: she was a different person than she had been three days ago. She kept her eyes on her own reflection, letting the whir of the camera become white noise as Umberto giggled to himself, moving the tip of the blade over her body, tickling her navel and then bringing it lower.

She would not give him the satisfaction of a response: she would ruin the movie by being an uncooperative, unemotional participant. A bad actor.

Before long, the camera dropped lower, focusing on the swell of her blouse instead of the blank expression she had willed to her face. He knew what she was trying to do, and it was making him agitated.

His giggle turned into a protracted growl as he poked at her thighs with the duller edge of the blade. She didn't look down, but she could feel the blood begin to dribble down her knee.

"You won't get what you want," she said, perfectly aware that he wouldn't understand. He took his eye from the viewfinder and stared at her, raising the machete high, letting her know that if she wouldn't cooperate, he would bring it down on her neck.

"Fuck you," she said. He probably knew that one, had most likely heard it directed at him by a thousand different women in a dozen different languages.

"No. Fuck you," he said, eye back behind the camera, arm reeled all the way back.

As he began to swing, there was a sound like a ceramic bowl breaking under a pillow. Umberto's eye went gloss, and behind it a light was switched off. He listed for a second, the weight of the camera pulling him over and down.

He collapsed, the back of his golden hair mottled with dark, sticky blood.

Jacque attempted to give him a second blow with the large rock, but he could not lift it with both hands. It thudded to the ground, landing in the small of Umberto's back.

"You're alive," Cynthia said. It seemed the only thing to say. Her surprise was genuine.

Jacque didn't speak. He stumbled towards her like a drunk, looking unaccustomed to using his feet and taking wide clumsy steps to get to her. Squishing her against the stake, he leaned into her for support while he undid the tape around her wrists.

She kissed his neck as he worked, but if he felt it, he gave no indication.

As he unwound the last piece, she fell a few inches back to solid footing. Her knees buckled, and they crumpled to the dirt together.

"Thank you," she said, and he nodded in response.

Umberto grunted, the camera still running in his hands.

Cynthia took hold of the solid piece of equipment. She'd never held one before. It was heavier than she imagined it would be. Either that, or her arms were that weak.

With one eye open, Umberto studied her, blood pooling in his ear and spilling over onto his cheek.

Without a word, she lifted the camera above her head and brought the back-end down on the side of his face. There was a crunch, and the veins in Umberto's arms and chest jumped as if electrified.

Before she knew that she had lifted it a second time, she brought the still-running camera down again on the place where his ear used to be.

The sun had risen overhead. She tried to imagine the picture that was burning its way onto the film right now. She was sure that there would be flashes of overexposure and lens flares as she raised the camera up and it caught the glint of the sun.

But as she brought the machine down again and again on Umberto's ruined skull, would the viewer catch a glimpse of her face? What would she look like? Would she be made beautiful by her ferocity, an Amazonian Goddess of war and vengeance?

Or would she just be that halfie girl from Queens, only with a swollen nose and broken teeth so she didn't look as pretty as she used to on the stage?

Would she ever let anyone see the film, so they would be able to answer those questions?

Chapter 26
Jacque

The sand was warm.

Jacque could tell that it was too warm for Cynthia, who shifted uncomfortably on top of it, finally unbuttoning her blouse and using it as a beach towel. For him, it was just right. It was getting more difficult to feel anything, so the warmth was a welcome sensation.

"It's going to be dark soon," she said, tilting her head up to the setting sun and then swiveling to look at the runway behind them. She had packed what little they were taking back with them in one of the empty crates, and walked it to the landing strip while he dozed on the beach during the afternoon.

Maybe 'dozed' was not the best way of describing it. 'Shivered until he lost consciousness' might have been more apt.

"The plane will hopefully be here in the morning," she said.

When she had helped him back to the beach, he could not stop saying "thank you," but now he was quiet. He had not been able to gather the strength to speak to her for a few hours now, but she kept calm and continued talking to him anyway.

"Although the way this trip has been going, I wouldn't be surprised if they were late," she continued, smiling down at him, resting her hand over his heart.

He wanted to feel it, but he couldn't.

After watching the sunset with her, he dipped back into sleep. He had more of those same dreams he had had while he was tied to the stake, but he was sure that they were beyond dreams this time.

There was no tunnel of white light. His grandparents and old pets weren't calling down to him from heaven. There was simply the feeling that he was somewhere else.

All around him, the people of the island waited. Some of them stood. Some of them paced up and down the beach. But the little old woman just crossed her backwards feet and sat next to him on the sand.

She placed her old gnarled hand on the other side of his chest.

He felt it.

"I'm truly sorry about this," she said. Through her touch, he saw it all: the curse, the massacre, the mass grave that they had uncovered in the jungle. All of it.

"It's all right," Jacque said, not sure if he was talking aloud in his sleep or just talking in the dream. "I'm going to have to stay here, on the island, aren't I?" he asked.

The old woman did not answer him. She just turned her head to look out over the ocean, up into the bluish-black sky, and watched as the stars began to blink themselves into existence.

Epilogue
The City

The black girl would have intimidated Roland—there was such intensity in her eyes—but there was something pitiful about them, too. She was covered in bandages and scars, limping into his office and looking like she hurt all over.

"Here's your fucking movie," she said, setting down a heavy package on Pressberg's desk. "The director says it is pure cinema. Whatever. I'm not even sure what that means. All I know is that now I get a percentage of the profits. I earned them."

Taking up the letter opener from his desk, Pressberg slit the tape on the package and lifted the flaps.

"Clothes?" he asked, lifting up a pair of floral patterned sundresses.

The girl snatched them out of his hands.

"I buried it deep, in case I got caught by customs." Under the bandages, she was a very pretty girl. But that voice: pure Queens, possibly the westernmost limits of Long Island.

"I was wondering when I'd be receiving this," he said to her, lifting up the first canister and reading the label. "Tito usually delivers these things himself. How did you say you got a hold of it?"

"I didn't steal it, if that's what you're insinuating. I'm the star," she said. "When can I be expecting a check?"

"*Tribesmen*…that's kind of generic. People won't even

know it's a horror picture. *The Tribe from Cannibal Hell*," Pressberg said, inspecting the title of the film and trying to avoid talking money with this girl. "Where is Tito? I haven't heard from the little toad in a week, which is unusual."

"Dead," the girl said, stone-faced. "He died making that movie. So did a lot of other people."

Pressberg put the top canister back in the box and stared back at the girl. After an uncomfortable moment, he smiled and began to laugh.

"You had me going there for a second," he said, reaching into his middle drawer for his checkbook. "Tell Tito I think that the gag is a wonderful idea: pretending to be dead to drum up some free publicity. Who should I be making this out to, Tito or yourself?"

"Make it to cash," she said.

"Oh, I get you. You're trying to limit the paper trail. A dead man shouldn't be cashing checks."

He started scribbling out an advance, plus a bonus for the stunt, but hesitated before handing it over. "Before you take this, one thing: make sure that you keep a low profile for a little while, too. Nobody will believe the trick if you show up in twenty of these kind of pictures over the next year. It will ruin the illusion."

"Don't worry," she said grabbing the check and tucking it into her handbag.

"I'm quitting the business."

Author's Afterword

In August of 2011, I sent the legendary John Skipp a direct message on Facebook and changed the entire trajectory of my life. Outside of a few choice memes, it might be the best thing Facebook has ever done for anyone.

At that point, I'd had a few short stories published and had finished up my first novel. Finished, but had no idea if the thing would ever be published. A few months prior to sending Skipp that message, I had graduated film school (a degree I nearly chickened out on, began overloading with English classes) and was pursuing a teaching degree. To say I was having a crisis of faith, freaking out over what I was going to do with my life, would be putting it mildly. I wanted to tell stories. More specifically, I wanted to tell horror stories. I enjoyed writing screenplays, but wasn't sure I wanted to gamble it all and move to Hollywood. I'd been in the horror fiction scene, but mostly as a fan. Until that day in August when Skipp posted an open call for "lean, mean novellas that can be read in about the same amount of time as a feature film."

That call for work sounded great to me and in about an hour I'd come up with the two sentence elevator pitch for Tribesmen. A pitch where I made it sound like this was a book I'd been working on already, was nearly finished with, had pages locked and loaded to send. But who cared if I was stretching the truth? I had plenty of time. Publishing moves glacially slow. So, with my pitch sent, I dusted off my hands, went to get dinner, and expected to hear back from Skipp sometime between 7-14 days and never. But I guess I didn't know who I was dealing with, because 29 minutes later (FB saves these details, even if it's over 7 years down the line), Skipp had written me back: interested.

What followed was a creative mad-dash, writing the book, working on the edits with Skipp, and having it beat my first novel (Video Night) to market by a few months. The first edition of Tribesmen sported a handsome cover from Paula Hanback and was part of a line that—while short-lived—consisted of some great books. A few years later, Skipp rescued the book from that publisher and brought it over to Deadite Press. I was over-joyed. Jeff Burk and Rose O'Keefe treated me well, getting the book a new life, a much bigger audience, and a Matthew Revert cover. Now, 7 years and three editions later (plus one in German! A now-defunct publisher who never even sent me copies!) I'm very happy to give Tribesmen one more home at Black T-Shirt Books. With another Revert cover and interior design by my friend (and the best freelancer at what he does, hire him) Scott Cole.

Looking back over the manuscript for this release, I still enjoy it, but I'm struck by how much of my anxiety at the time colors this book and its attitudes towards films and filmmaking. Even when I wrote this and Video Night, I didn't think that books would be the answer. That books would be the thing to keep the lights on, to get me jobs teaching, speaking, writing comics, that Tribesmen would cross someone's desk at Random House and get me my first "big budget" book, and—fingers crossed—pull me back into the world of film. No, I wrote books because I love books, I love horror, and I wanted to tell stories.

Without John Skipp's encouragement, mentorship, and lightning fast message response time, there wouldn't be a Tribes-men. But without you buying, recommending, reviewing, or otherwise supporting these books: there wouldn't be an Adam

Cesare. Not sure I can put into words how much I owe you.

Thank you,
Adam
12/11/2018

Want More Cesare? Read on to get your fix:

Download a FREE exclusive ebook
by visiting www.adamcesare.com

The Blackest Eyes is a mini collection of two short stories. This ebook is free for everyone who signs up for *Adam Cesare's Mailing List of Terror*.

What are you Waiting for? Go to AdamCesare.com and sign up today!

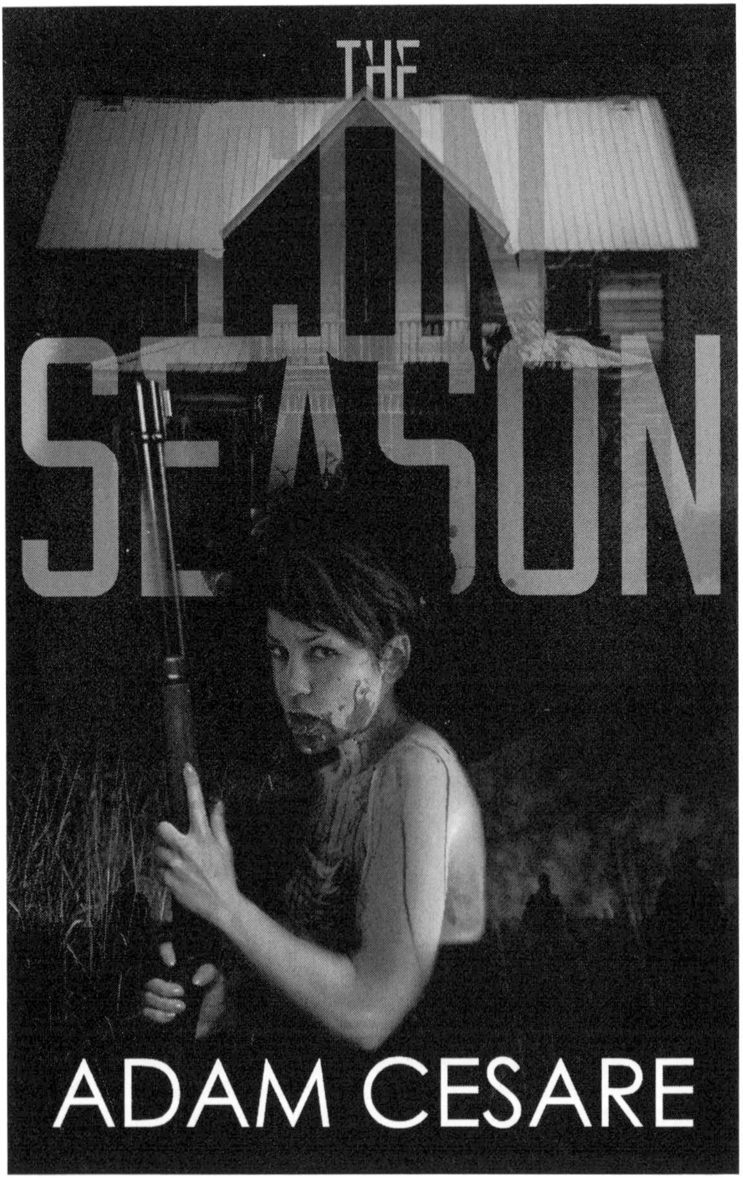
THE
SEASON
ADAM CESARE

Also Available:

The Con Season

Horror movie starlet Clarissa Lee is beautiful, internationally known, and…completely broke.

To cap off years of questionable financial and personal decisions, Clarissa accepts an invitation to participate in a "fully immersive" fan convention. She arrives at an off-season summer camp and finds what was supposed to be a quick buck has become a real-life slasher movie.

Deep in the woods of Kentucky with a supporting cast of B-level celebrities, Clarissa must fight to survive the deadly game that the con's organizers have rigged against her.

A demented, funny, bloody, and strangely-poignant horror novel.

**Available now in ebook,
paperback, and audiobook.**

THE SUMMER JOB

ADAM CESARE

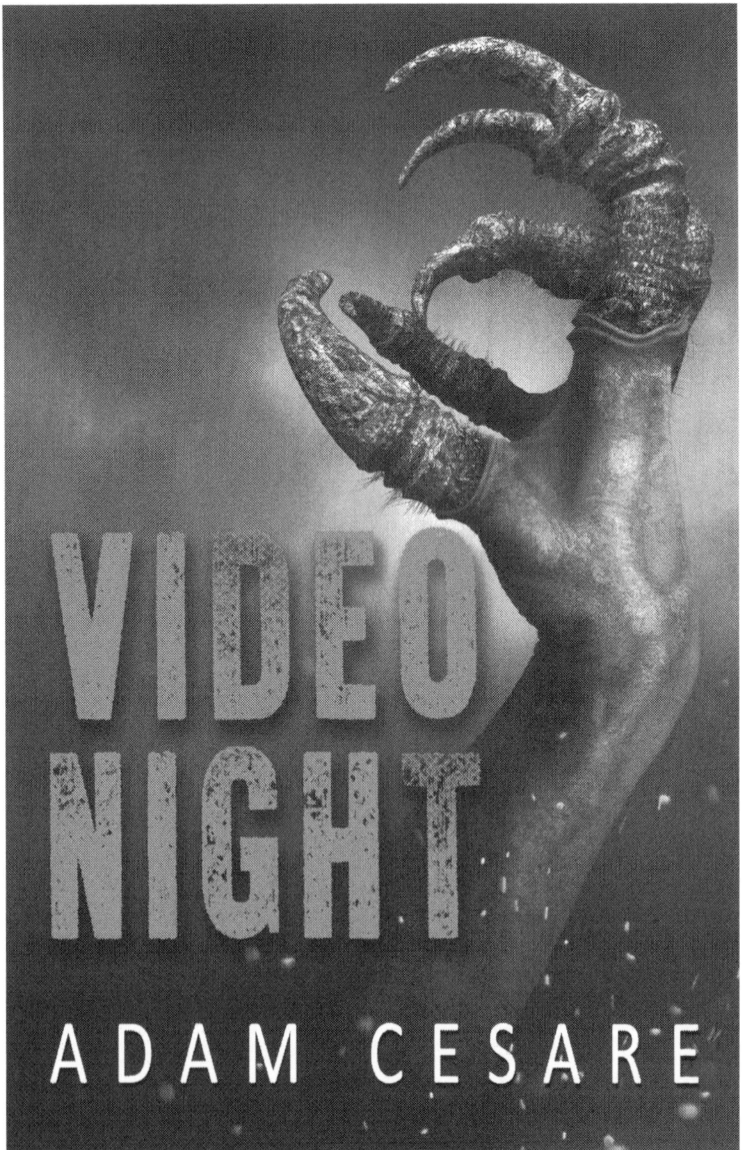
VIDEO
NIGHT
ADAM CESARE

THE FIRST ONE YOU EXPECT

YOU EXPECT

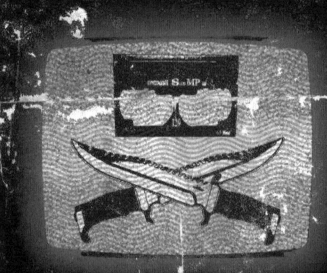

ADAM CESARE

MERCY
HOUSE

ADAM CESARE

Mercy House

"Adam Cesare's *Mercy House* is a rowdy, gory, blood-soaked horror tale guaranteed to keep you up at night. And if that was all it was, I'd have been a happy reader. But Cesare has a maturity far and away beyond his years. His characters are treated with a surprising capacity for understanding and empathy, giving them an unexpected depth rarely seen among the nightmare crowd. *Mercy House* is the kind of novel you sprint through, eating up the pages as fast as you can turn them, and yet it lingers in the mind like a haunting memory, or the ghost of a smell. Cesare is poised to take the reins of the new generation. Looking for the new face of horror? This is it right here."—**Joe McKinney, Bram Stoker Award–winning author of *The Dead Won't Die* and *Dead City***

"*Mercy House* is 100% distilled nightmare juice. Adam Cesare notches up the horror to nigh-unbearable levels. Even my skin was screaming by the end of this book."—**Nick Cutter, author of *The Troop***

"Adam Cesare makes his presence felt with *Mercy House*. A no-holds-barred combo of survival horror and the occult."—**Laird Barron, author of *The Beautiful Thing That Awaits Us All***

"This is extreme horror at its best, so don't step into this book with an uneasy stomach. You must wait sixty minutes after eating before opening up *Mercy House*."—***LitReactor***

**This novel is available as an ebook
from Random House Hydra.**

EXPONENTIAL

ADAM CESARE

THE ARCADE SCENE
ISN'T DEAD...IT'S ALIVE!
ZERO
LIVES REMAINING
ADAM CESARE

About the Author

Adam Cesare is a New Yorker who lives in Philadelphia.

His work has been featured in numerous magazines and anthologies. His nonfiction has appeared in *Paracinema*, *The LA Review of Books* and other venues. He also writes a monthly column about the intersection of horror fiction and film for *Cemetery Dance Online*.

His novels and novellas are available in ebook and paperback from Amazon, Barnes & Noble, and all other fine retailers.

Please visit his website adamcesare.com to learn more. Author photo by John Urbancik.

Printed in Poland
by Amazon Fulfillment
Poland Sp. z o.o., Wrocław